LITTLE DOROTHY AND TOTO
ARE IN BIG TROUBLE!

"Silence!" roared a great voice, and Dorothy opened her eyes to find that the tiny man had suddenly grown to a giant and was holding both her and Toto in a tight embrace while in one step he spanned the lake and reached the other shore.

"Stop!" she screamed. "Who are you, and where are you taking me?" The giant said not a word.

Close to Dorothy's ear, however, a voice answered her, saying: "This is the terrible Crinklink, and he has you in his power."

Dorothy managed to twist her head around and found it was the second button on the jacket—the wolf's head—which had spoken to her.

"What will Crinklink do with me?" she asked anxiously.

"No one knows. You must wait and see," replied the wolf.

"Some of his captives he whips," squeaked the weasel's head.

"Some he transforms into bugs, and other things," growled the bear's head.

"Some he enchants, so that they become doorknobs," sighed the cat's head.

"Some he makes his slaves—even as we are—and that is the most dreadful fate of all," added the field-mouse. "As long as Crinklink exists we shall remain buttons, but as there are no more buttonholes on his jacket he will probably make you a slave. . . ."

Other Bantam Skylark Books you will enjoy
Ask your bookseller for the books you have missed

Little Wizard Stories
of Oz

By L. Frank Baum

Introduction by
Michael Patrick Hearn

—

Illustrated by John R. Neill

—

A BANTAM SKYLARK BOOK®
TORONTO · NEW YORK · LONDON · SYDNEY · AUCKLAND

RL 6, 008–012

THIS EDITION CONTAINS THE COMPLETE TEXT
OF THE ORIGINAL HARDCOVER EDITION.
NOT ONE WORD HAS BEEN OMITTED.

LITTLE WIZARD STORIES OF OZ
A Bantam Skylark Book / published by arrangement with Schocken Books

PRINTING HISTORY
Schocken Books edition published November 1985,
copyright © 1985 by the Baum Trust.
Bantam edition / October 1988
Skylark Books is a registered trademark of Bantam Books, a division of Bantam Doubleday Dell Publishing Group, Inc. Registered in U.S. Patent and Trademark Office and elsewhere.

Library of Congress Catalog Card Number: 85-10753.

For information address: Schocken Books, a division of Random House, Inc., 201 East 50th Street, New York, NY, 10022.

ISBN 0-553-15617-9

Published simultaneously in the United States and Canada

Bantam Books are published by Bantam Books, a division of Bantam Doubleday Dell Publishing Group, Inc. Its trademark, consisting of the words "Bantam Books" and the portrayal of a rooster, is Registered in U.S. Patent and Trademark Office and in other countries. Marca Registrada. Bantam Books, 666 Fifth Avenue, New York, New York 10103.

PRINTED IN THE UNITED STATES OF AMERICA

S 0 9 8 7 6 5 4 3 2 1

CONTENTS

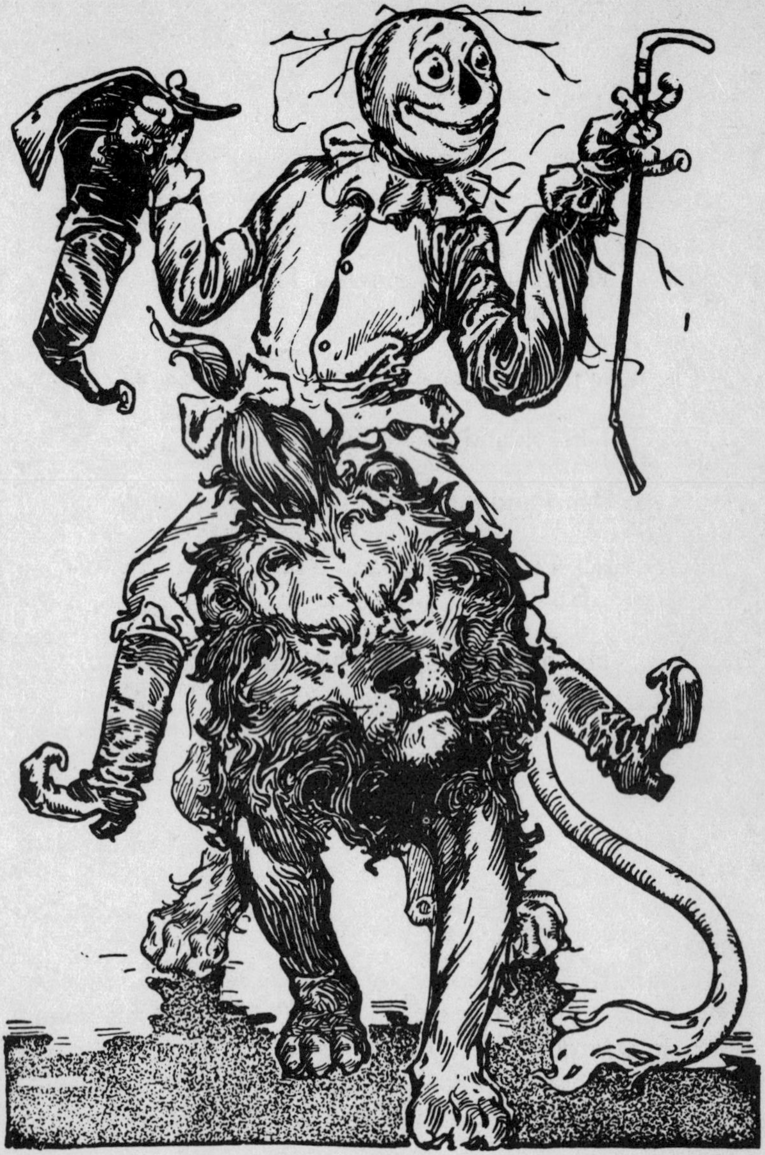

INTRODUCTION

When L. Frank Baum and W. W. Denslow published *The Wonderful Wizard of Oz* with the George M. Hill Company of Chicago in 1900, the author and his artist did not at first fully comprehend the significance of this American fairy tale free of all heartaches and nightmares. "Then there is the other book, the best thing I ever have written, they tell me, *The Wonderful Wizard of Oz*," Baum modestly wrote his brother that spring. "Mr. Hill, the publisher, says he expects a sale of at least a quarter of a million copies on it. . . . But the queer, unreliable Public has not yet spoken." That queer, unreliable Public replied immediately, by making *The Wonderful Wizard of Oz* the best-selling children's book of the year, and in 1902, when it became the basis of a highly successful musical extravaganza, the book's success was secure.

Originally Baum had no intention of writing a sequel to *The Wizard of Oz*. For several years he ignored his young readers' entreaties for "more about Oz, Mr. Baum." He had parted with his illustrator, and his publisher had gone bankrupt, the rights to *The Wizard of Oz* being transferred to another house. However, Frank K. Reilly and Sumner C. Britton, formerly with the defunct Hill firm, convinced Baum to write further adventures of the Scarecrow and the Tin Woodman and secured for him a new illustrator, the young Philadelphia newspaper cartoonist John R. Neill. In 1904, they formed their own publishing house, the Reilly & Britton Company, to issue *The Marvelous Land of Oz*, and the second Oz book proved to be nearly as successful as the first. Baum then signed an exclusive contract with Reilly & Britton and produced six titles in the series before he grew weary of Oz. He said he had other fairy tales to write. Therefore, in 1910, in *The Emerald City of Oz*, Baum abruptly tried to end the series with a sad note from Dorothy: "You will never hear anything more about Oz, because we are now cut off forever from the rest of the world. But Toto and I will always love you and all the other children who love us."

But forever is a long time. In 1911 and 1912, Baum published two of his finest stories, *The Sea Fairies* and *Sky Island*, but sales of these books were disappointing. All the children wanted was "more about Oz, Mr. Baum." The author was finally forced to return to Oz: Having declared bankruptcy in 1911 due to an unsuccessful motion picture project, Baum now had to comply with their wishes. In 1913 he resumed the series with one of his best books, *The Patchwork Girl of Oz*.

The publishers assured the writer that they were going to inaugurate a "large promotion of L. Frank Baum and all of his books for the year 1913." An important part of this campaign was the publication of "The Little Wizard Series," six short Oz adventures by Baum, which Reilly & Britton first issued in 1913 in individual volumes and then as a collection in 1914 as *The Little Wizard Stories of Oz*. In addition to Dorothy, the Scarecrow, the Tin Woodman, the Cowardly Lion, and Oz himself from *The Wizard of Oz*, these fairy tales featured such popular Baum characters as Jack Pumpkinhead and the Sawhorse from *The Marvelous Land of Oz* and Ozma, the Hungry Tiger, Tik-Tok, and the Nome King from *Ozma of Oz*. Baum admitted that "in writing these stories I did not want . . . to use material that would be of value in my future Oz stories." Clearly these six charming narratives were designed for a slightly younger audience than that of the standard Oz stories, and were filled with adventures just right for bedtime.

Ever mindful of their author's reputation and intentions, the publishers required some revisions of the manuscripts Baum sent them on September 23, 1912. They were especially careful in the preparation of these short Oz stories, for they hoped to serialize them in *The Ladies' Home Journal*, *The Woman's Home Companion*, or one of the other major mass-market women's magazines before their appearance in book form. Britton diplomatically suggested that in the first version of "The Scarecrow and the Tin Woodman" Baum may not have done "justice to these two great characters that have won fame and fortune. . . . It was one of the first stories you submitted and while it is sweet and pretty yet it is not an astonishing tale the same as the other five will be." Baum welcomed this criticism and immediately wrote another story about the Scarecrow and the Tin Woodman, adding that if the publishers did not like the new one, he would try again.

Britton was also distressed with "Little Dorothy and Toto" as originally written. He objected to the dog's disposal of the villain "on much the same order as a terrier would kill a rat." "This is clearly away from your usual style of not doing any killing," Britton continued, "and while this is no 'killing' matter, yet we think it well to live up to your reputation. Far be it for me to suggest any way to make a change in this story. However, a little thought occurred to me and I will submit it to you for what it is worth. Why could you not, after reducing Crinklink to a very small person . . . suddenly have Crinklink grow larger again and appear in the person of the Little Wizard of Oz, who would laugh heartily at the joke perpetrated on little Dorothy?" An added advantage of the new denouement was that in reintroducing the Wizard, it kept the story in line with the series' title. Again Baum good-naturedly embraced his friend and publisher's revision. "Your suggestion," he assured Britton, "was so excellent that I grabbed it straightway. You will find in the new writing . . . that the story is greatly strengthened and now wholly innocent of nightmares."

Baum was amused by his publishers' objection to another of the tales. While admitting that the manuscript of "Tik-Tok and the Nome King" was "bully and full of ginger right from the start," Britton went on to say that the use of "murder" and "ghosts" in the story might "be considered a grave departure from the regular way of L. Frank Baum and his fairy stories. . . . Ghosts are not for the very little tots that this story will reach and I am afraid that our slogan that 'no Baum story ever sent a child to bed to troubled dreams' will be put out of business." "In spite of my deep veneration and reverence for your wisdom, old top," Baum immediately replied, "you made me laugh when you objected to Tik-Tok's 'ghost' and the 'murder' of a clockwork man! . . . All honor to the Great Baum, who has made his machine man so real and life-like that even his publisher is horrified by the suggestion that the clockworks has a ghost and might haunt its smasher!" Nevertheless, fearful that "the youngsters might also miss my occult humor and have bad dreams about Tik-Tok's murder and ghost," Baum carefully cleansed his tale of any possibly disturbing detail.

Nothing remains in the six published stories which might trouble a child's sleep. Even the rusting of the Tin Woodman and the smashing of Jack's pumpkinhead are quickly corrected by the Little Wizard; the Cowardly Lion and the Hungry Tiger turn out to be not so fierce as they first appear to be. These slight, lighthearted romps through Baum's fairyland are harmless, tongue-in-cheek episodes from the saga of Oz. The little lessons to be learned in "The Little Wizard Stories," such as do not lose your temper like the Nome King or do not wander off alone like Dorothy, never carry some fearsome moral as do those in the fairy tales of Grimm and Andersen. And Baum tempers his adventures with humor, particularly with puns. The naughty crows agree to help the Tin Woodman "all together for the good caws"; and Baum was so proud of the names Imp Olite, Imp Udent, and Imp Ertinent that he later introduced variants of them in *The Uplift of Lucifer*, a play he put on for a men's club he belonged to in California.

At first Baum had objected to the publishers' decision to have John R. Neill, who had illustrated all of the Oz books but *The Wizard of Oz*, embellish "The Little Wizard Stories," because, their author felt, "Neill has not been giving satisfaction to my readers lately." Fortunately Reilly & Britton did not listen to the "Great Baum" in this instance, and Neill brightened the little books with some of his funniest pictures, all in full color. These stories are indeed, as the publishers advertised them, true "Oz books in miniature." No doubt Baum was finally pleased with Neill's admirable efforts in these little tales. And surely Baum would be happy to see all six of his long-forgotten "Little Wizard Stories" now together again in a single volume, with all of the original pictures, ready to delight a whole new generation of young readers of Oz.

MICHAEL PATRICK HEARN

THE COWARDLY LION
and
THE HUNGRY TIGER

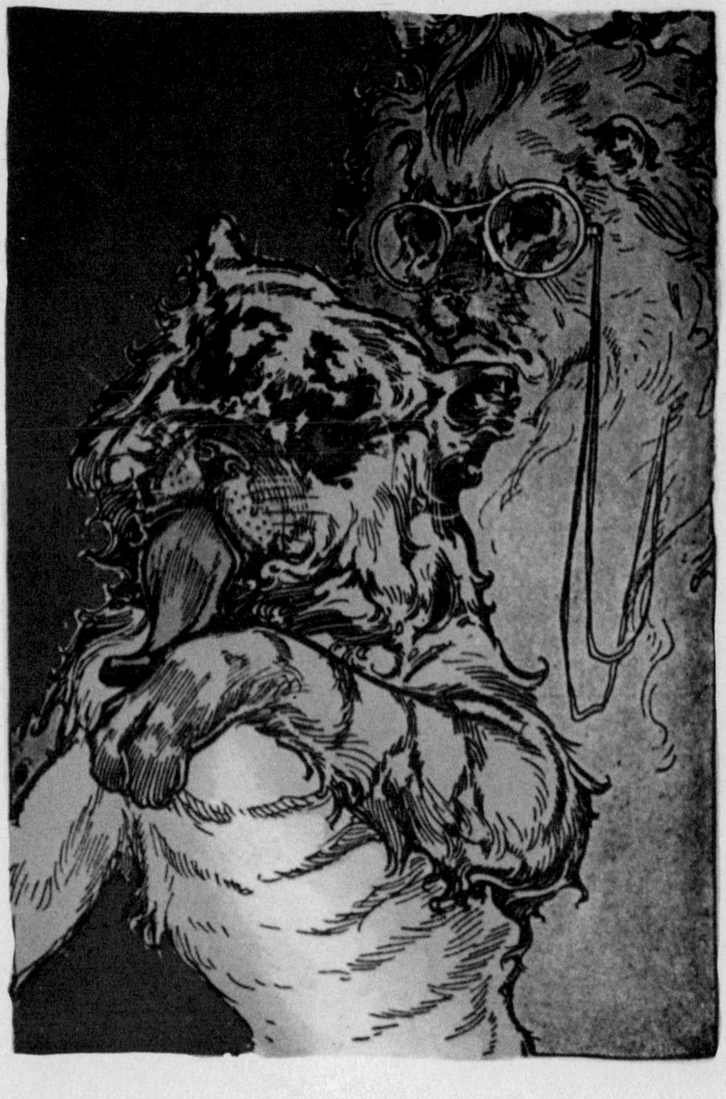

THE COWARDLY LION AND THE HUNGRY TIGER

I N the splendid palace of the Emerald City, which is in the center of the fairy Land of Oz, is a great Throne Room, where Princess Ozma, the Ruler, for an hour each day sits in a throne of glistening emeralds and listens to all the troubles of her people, which they are sure to tell her about. Around Ozma's throne, on such occasions, are grouped all the important personages of Oz, such as the Scarecrow, Jack Pumpkinhead, Tik-Tok the Clockwork Man, the Tin Woodman, the Wizard of Oz, the Shaggy Man, and other famous fairy people. Little Dorothy usually has a seat at Ozma's feet, and crouched on either side of the throne are two enormous beasts known as the Hungry Tiger and the Cowardly Lion.

These two beasts are Ozma's chief guardians, but as everyone loves the beautiful girl Princess there has never been any disturbance in the great Throne Room, or anything for the guardians to do but look fierce and solemn and keep quiet until the Royal Audience is over and the people go away to their homes.

Of course no one would dare be naughty while the huge Lion and Tiger crouched beside the throne; but the fact is, the people of Oz are very seldom naughty. So Ozma's big guards are more ornamental than useful, and no one realizes that better than the beasts themselves.

One day, after everybody had left the Throne Room except the Cowardly Lion and the Hungry Tiger, the Lion yawned and said to his friend:

"I'm getting tired of this job. No one is afraid of us and no one pays any attention to us."

"That is true," replied the big Tiger, purring softly. "We might as well be in the thick jungles where we were born, as trying to protect Ozma when she needs no protection. And I'm dreadfully hungry all the time."

"You have enough to eat, I'm sure," said the Lion, swaying his tail slowly back and forth.

"Enough, perhaps; but not the kind of food I long for," answered the Tiger. "What I'm hungry for is fat babies. I have a great desire to eat a few fat babies. Then, perhaps, the people of Oz would fear me and I'd become more important."

"True," agreed the Lion. "It would stir up quite a rumpus if you ate but *one* fat baby. As for myself, my claws are sharp as needles and strong as crowbars, while my teeth are powerful enough to tear a person to pieces in a few seconds. If I should spring upon a man and make chop suey of him, there would be wild excitement in the Emerald City and the people would fall upon their knees and beg me for mercy. That, in my opinion, would render me of considerable importance."

"After you had torn the person to pieces, what would you do next?" asked the Tiger sleepily.

"Then I would roar so loudly it would shake the earth and stalk away to the jungle to hide myself, before anyone could attack me or kill me for what I had done."

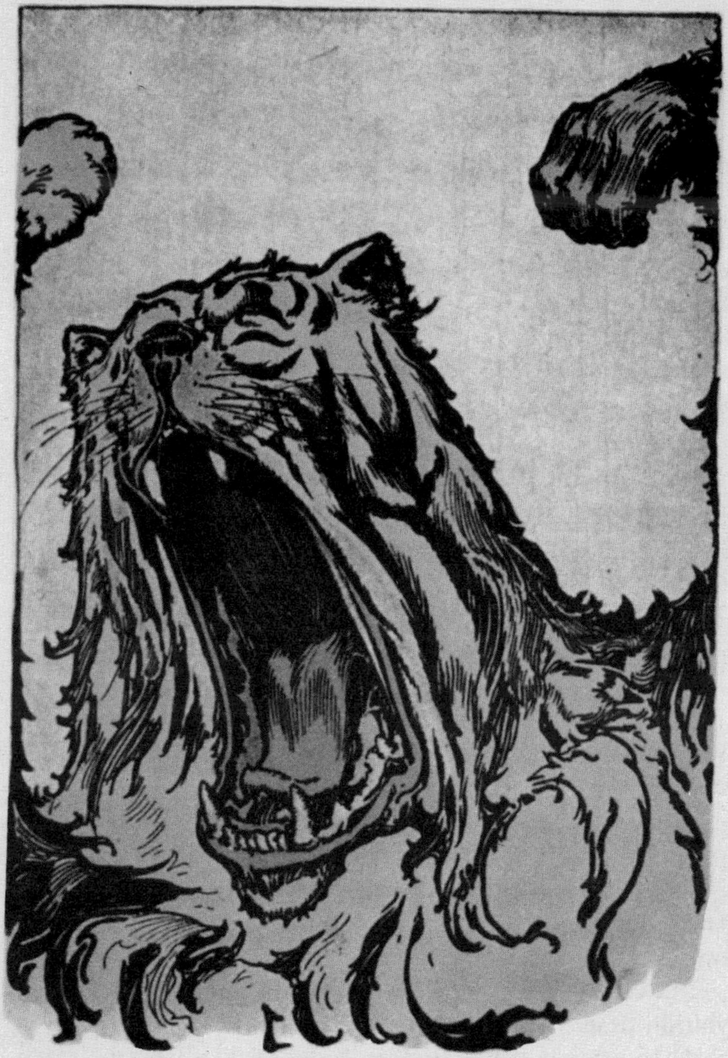

"I see," nodded the Tiger. "You are really cowardly."

"To be sure. That is why I am named the Cowardly Lion. That is why I have always been so tame and peaceful. But I'm awfully tired of being tame," added the Lion, with a sigh, "and it would be fun to raise a row and show people what a terrible beast I really am."

The Tiger remained silent for several minutes, thinking deeply as he slowly washed his face with his left paw. Then he said:

"I'm getting old, and it would please me to eat at least one fat baby before I die. Suppose we surprise these people of Oz and prove our power. What do you say? We will walk out of here just as usual and the first baby we meet I'll eat in a jiffy, and the first man or woman you meet you will tear to pieces. Then we will both run out of the city gates and gallop across the country and hide in the jungle before anyone can stop us."

"All right; I'm game," said the Lion, yawning again so that he showed two rows of dreadfully sharp teeth.

The Tiger got up and stretched his great, sleek body.

"Come on," he said. The Lion stood up and proved he was the larger of the two, for he was almost as big as a small horse.

Out of the palace they walked, and met no one. They passed through the beautiful grounds, past fountains and beds of lovely flowers, and met no one. Then they un-latched a gate and entered a street of the city, and met no one.

"I wonder how a fat baby will taste," remarked the Tiger, as they stalked majestically along, side by side.

"I imagine it will taste like nutmegs," said the Lion.

"No," said the Tiger, "I've an idea it will taste like gumdrops."

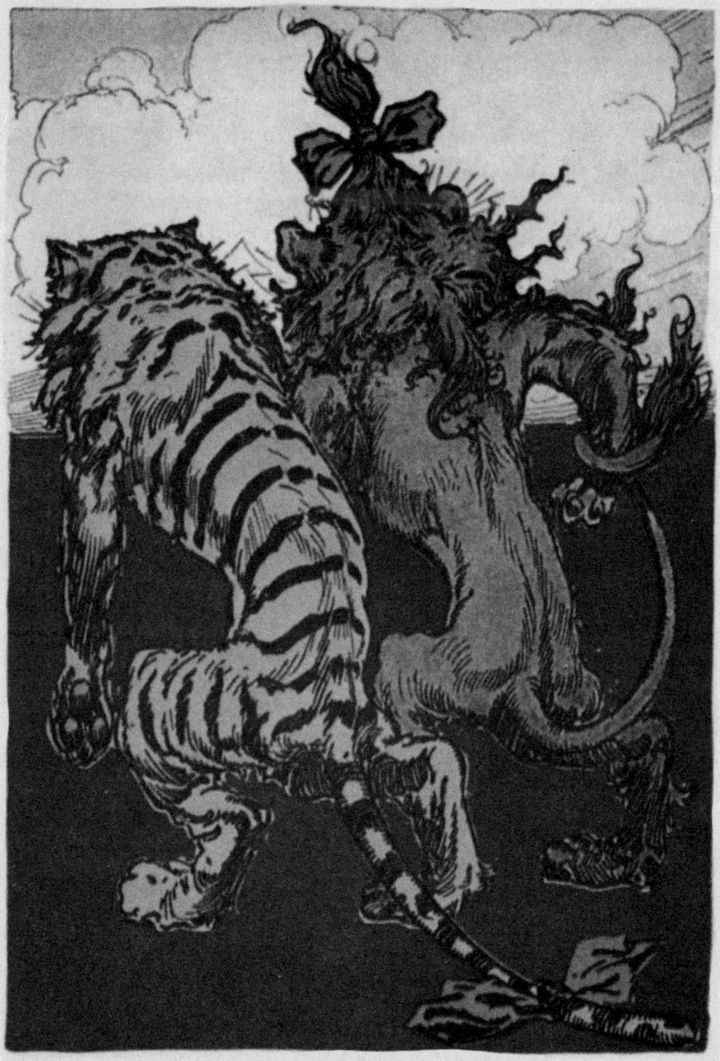

They turned a corner, but met no one, for the people of the Emerald City were accustomed to take their naps at this hour of the afternoon.

"I wonder how many pieces I ought to tear a person into," said the Lion, in a thoughtful voice.

"Sixty would be about right," suggested the Tiger.

"Would that hurt any more than to tear one into about a dozen pieces?" inquired the Lion, with a little shudder.

"Who cares whether it hurts or not?" growled the Tiger.

The Lion did not reply. They entered a side street, but met no one.

Suddenly they heard a child crying.

"Aha!" exclaimed the Tiger. "There is my meat."

He rushed around a corner, the Lion following, and came upon a nice fat baby sitting in the middle of the street and crying as if in great distress.

"What's the matter?" asked the Tiger, crouching before the baby.

"I—I—l-lost my m-m-mamma!" wailed the baby.

"Why, you poor little thing," said the great beast, softly stroking the child's head with its paw. "Don't cry, my dear, for mamma can't be far away and I'll help you to find her."

"Go on," said the Lion, who stood by.

"Go on where?" asked the Tiger, looking up.

"Go on and eat your fat baby."

"Why, you dreadful creature!" said the Tiger reproachfully; "would you want me to eat a poor little lost baby, that don't know where its mother is?" And the beast gathered the little one into its strong, hairy arms and tried to comfort it by rocking it gently back and forth.

The Lion growled low in his throat and seemed very much disappointed; but at that moment a scream reached their ears and a woman came bounding out of a house and

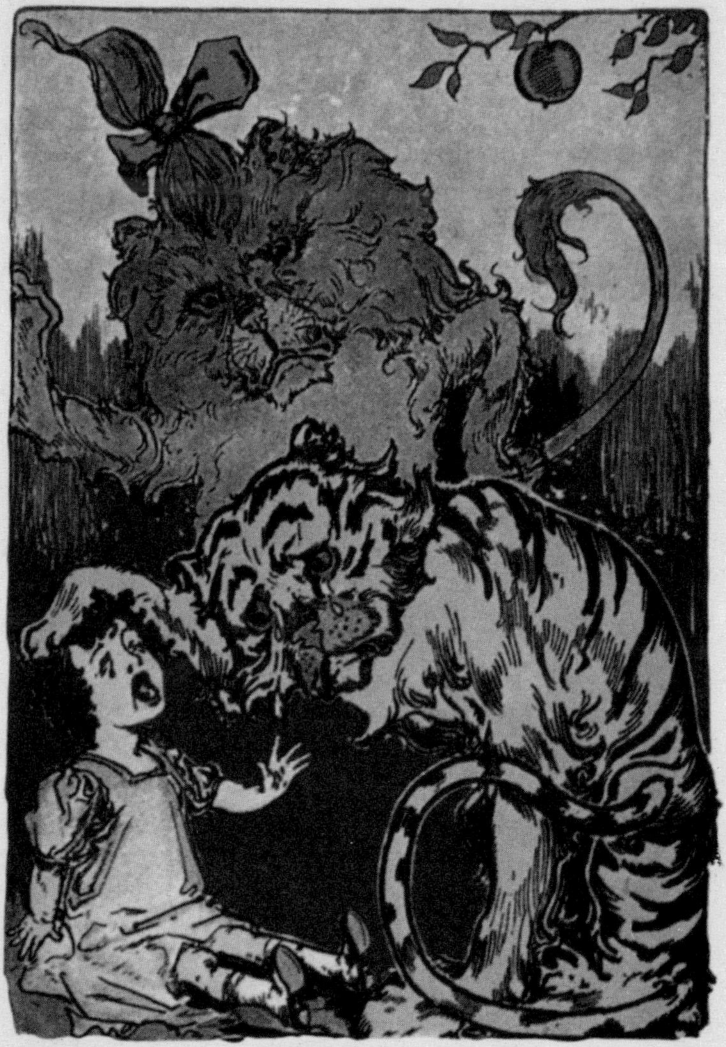

into the street. Seeing her baby in the embrace of the monster Tiger the woman screamed again and rushed forward to rescue it, but in her haste she caught her foot in her skirt and tumbled head over heels and heels over head, stopping with such a bump that she saw many stars in the heavens, although it was broad daylight. And there she lay, in a helpless manner, all tangled up and unable to stir.

With one bound and a roar like thunder the huge Lion was beside her. With his strong jaws he grasped her dress and raised her into an upright position.

"Poor thing! Are you hurt?" he gently asked.

Gasping for breath the woman struggled to free herself and tried to walk, but she limped badly and tumbled down again.

"My baby!" she said pleadingly.

"The baby is all right; don't worry," replied the Lion; and then he added: "Keep quiet, now, and I'll carry you back to your house, and the Hungry Tiger will carry your baby."

The Tiger, which had approached the place with the child in its arms, asked in astonishment:

"Aren't you going to tear her into sixty pieces?"

"No, nor into six pieces," answered the Lion indignantly. "I'm not such a brute as to destroy a poor woman who has hurt herself trying to save her lost baby. If you are so ferocious and cruel and bloodthirsty, you may leave me and go away, for I do not care to associate with you."

"That's all right," answered the Tiger. "I'm not cruel— not in the least—I'm only hungry. But I thought *you* were cruel."

"Thank heaven I'm respectable," said the Lion, with dignity. He then raised the woman and with much gentleness carried her into her house, where he laid her upon a sofa.

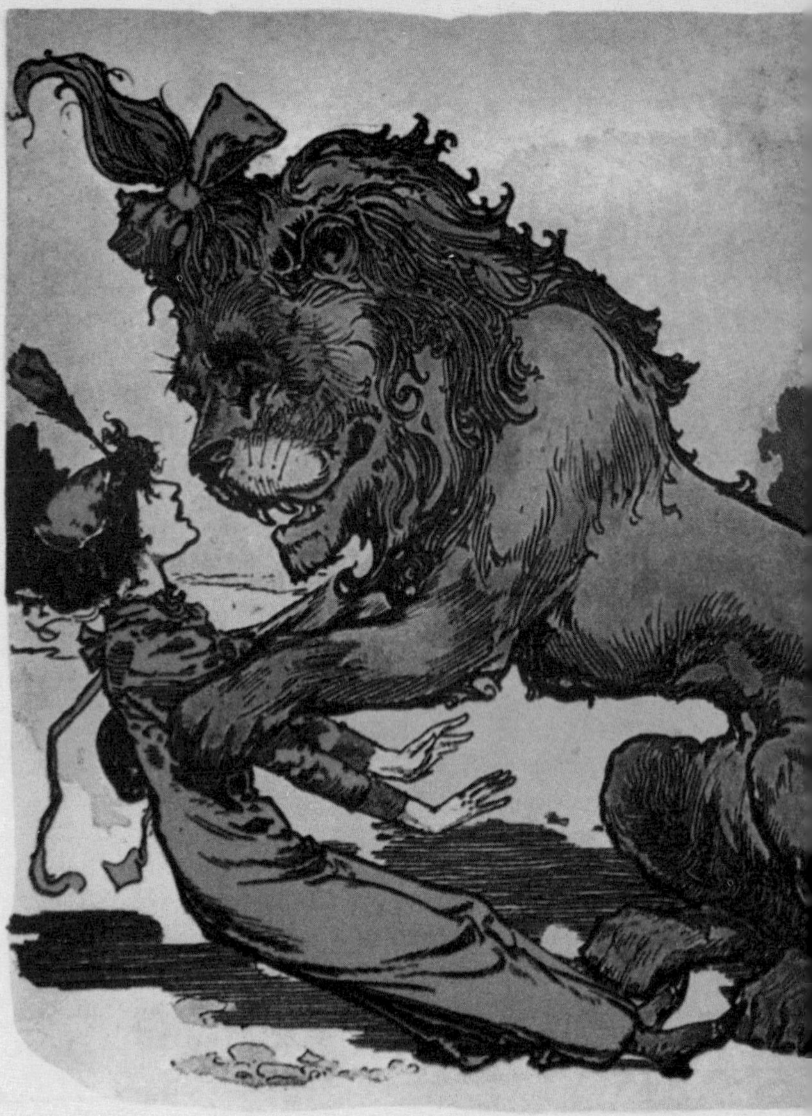

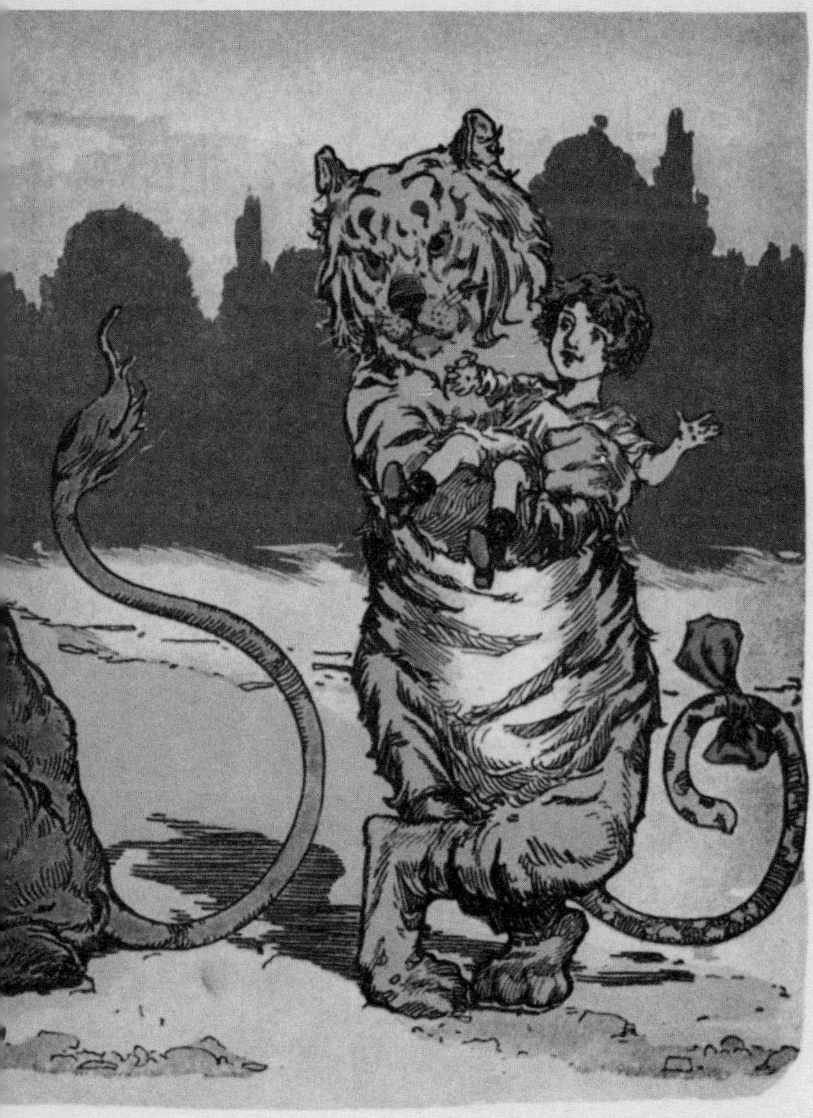

The Tiger followed with the baby, which he safely deposited beside its mother. The little one liked the Hungry Tiger and grasping the enormous beast by both ears the baby kissed the beast's nose to show he was grateful and happy.

"Thank you very much," said the woman. "I've often heard what good beasts you are, in spite of your power to do mischief to mankind, and now I know that the stories are true. I do not think either of you have ever had an evil thought."

The Hungry Tiger and the Cowardly Lion hung their heads and did not look into each other's eyes, for both were shamed and humbled. They crept away and stalked back through the streets until they again entered the palace grounds, where they retreated to the pretty, comfortable rooms they occupied at the back of the palace. There they silently crouched in their usual corners to think over their recent adventure.

After a while the Tiger said sleepily:

"I don't believe fat babies taste like gumdrops. I'm quite sure they have the flavor of raspberry tarts. My, how hungry I am for fat babies!"

The Lion grunted disdainfully.

"You're a humbug," said he.

"Am I?" retorted the Tiger, with a sneer. "Tell me, then, into how many pieces you usually tear your victims, my bold Lion?"

The Lion impatiently thumped the floor with his tail.

"To tear anyone into pieces would soil my claws and blunt my teeth," he said. "I'm glad I didn't muss myself up this afternoon by hurting that poor mother."

The Tiger looked at him steadily and then yawned a wide, wide yawn.

"You're a coward," he remarked.

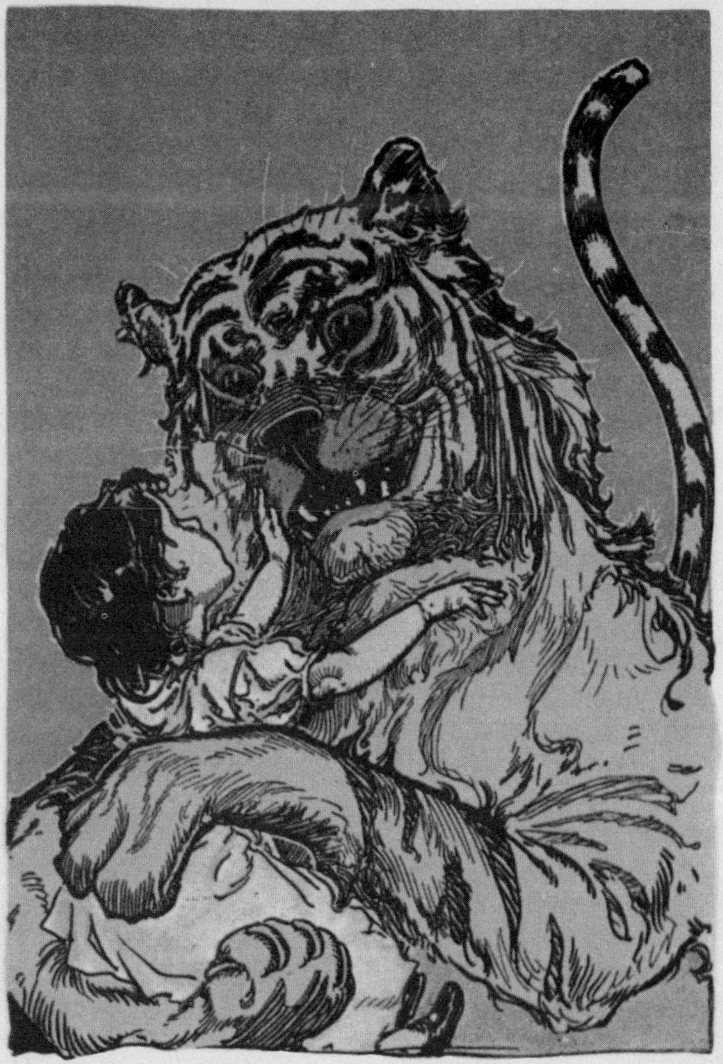

"Well," said the Lion, "it's better to be a coward than to do wrong."

"To be sure," answered the other. "And that reminds me that I nearly lost my own reputation. For, had I eaten that fat baby, I would not now be the Hungry Tiger. It's better to go hungry, seems to me, than to be cruel to a little child."

And then they dropped their heads on their paws and went to sleep.

LITTLE DOROTHY
and
TOTO

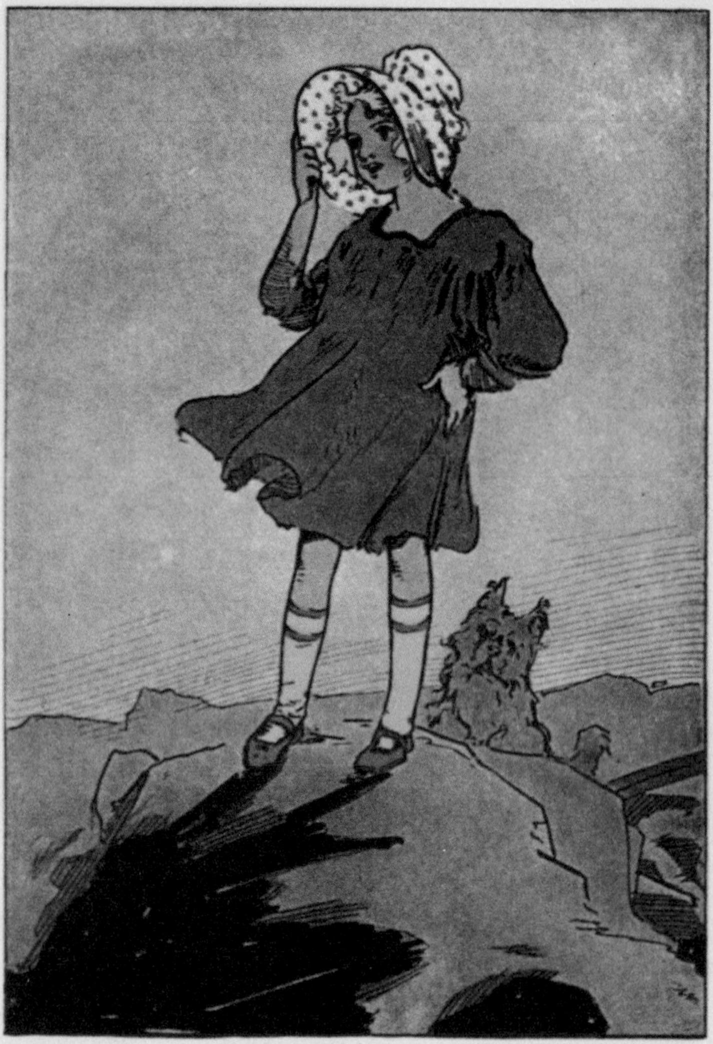

LITTLE DOROTHY AND TOTO

DOROTHY was a little Kansas girl who once accidentally found the beautiful Land of Oz and was invited to live there always. Toto was Dorothy's small black dog, with fuzzy, curly hair and bright black eyes. Together, when they tired of the grandeur of the Emerald City of Oz, they would wander out into the country and all through the land, peering into queer nooks and corners and having a good time in their own simple way. There was a little Wizard living in Oz who was a faithful friend of Dorothy and did not approve of her traveling alone in this way, but the girl always laughed at the little man's fears for her and said she was not afraid of anything that might happen.

One day, while on such a journey, Dorothy and Toto found themselves among the wild wooded hills at the southeast of Oz—a place usually avoided by travelers because so many magical things abounded there. And, as they entered a forest path, the little girl noticed a sign tacked to a tree, which said: "Look out for Crinklink."

Toto could not talk, as many of the animals of Oz can, for he was just a common Kansas dog; but he looked at the sign so seriously that Dorothy almost believed he could read it, and she knew quite well that Toto understood every word she said to him.

"Never mind Crinklink," said she. "I don't believe anything in Oz will try to hurt us, Toto, and if I get into trouble you must take care of me."

"Bow-wow!" said Toto, and Dorothy knew that meant a promise.

The path was narrow and wound here and there between the trees, but they could not lose their way, because thick vines and creepers shut them in on both sides. They had walked a long time when, suddenly turning a curve of the pathway, they came upon a lake of black water, so big and so deep that they were forced to stop.

"Well, Toto," said Dorothy, looking at the lake, "we must turn back, I guess, for there is neither a bridge nor a boat to take us across the black water."

"Here's the ferryman, though," cried a tiny voice beside them, and the girl gave a start and looked down at her feet, where a man no taller than three inches sat at the edge of the path with his legs dangling over the lake.

"Oh!" said Dorothy; "I didn't see you before."

Toto growled fiercely and made his ears stand up straight, but the little man did not seem in the least afraid of the dog. He merely repeated: "I'm the ferryman, and it's my business to carry people across the lake."

Dorothy couldn't help feeling surprised, for she could have picked the little man up with one hand, and the lake was big and broad. Looking at the ferryman more closely she saw that he had small eyes, a big nose and a sharp chin. His hair was blue and his clothes scarlet, and Dorothy noticed that every button on his jacket was the head of some animal. The top button was a bear's head and the next button a wolf's head; the next was a cat's head and the next a

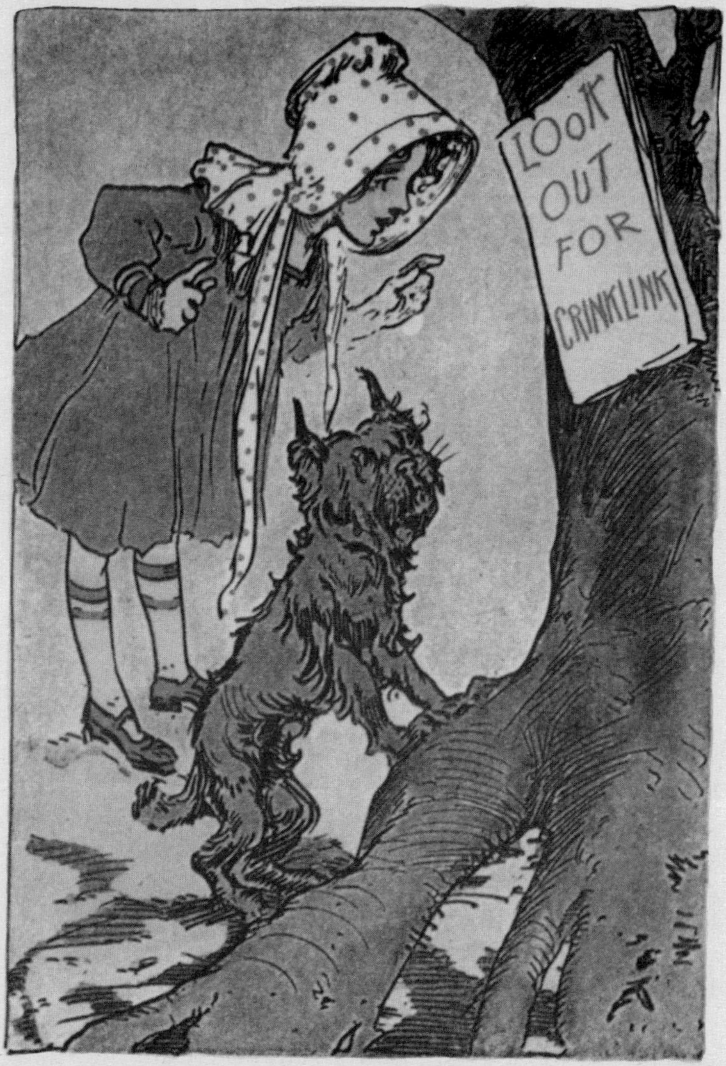
LOOK OUT FOR CRINKLINK

weasel's head, while the last button of all was the head of a
field-mouse. When Dorothy looked into the eyes of these
animals' heads, they all nodded and said in a chorus: "Don't
believe all you hear, little girl!"

"Silence!" said the small ferryman, slapping each button
head in turn, but not hard enough to hurt them. Then he
turned to Dorothy and asked: "Do you wish to cross over
the lake?"

"Why, I'd like to," she answered, hesitating; "but I can't
see how you will manage to carry us, without any boat."

"If you can't see, you mustn't see," he answered with a
laugh. "All you need do is shut your eyes, say the word,
and—over you go!"

Dorothy wanted to get across, in order that she might
continue her journey.

"All right," she said, closing her eyes; "I'm ready."

Instantly she was seized in a pair of strong arms—arms
so big and powerful that she was startled and cried out in
fear.

"Silence!" roared a great voice, and the girl opened her
eyes to find that the tiny man had suddenly grown to a giant
and was holding both her and Toto in a tight embrace while
in one step he spanned the lake and reached the other shore.

Dorothy became frightened, then, especially as the giant
did not stop but continued tramping in great steps over the
wooded hills, crushing bushes and trees beneath his broad
feet. She struggled in vain to free herself, while Toto
whined and trembled beside her, for the little dog was
frightened, too.

"Stop!" screamed the girl. "Let me down!" But the giant
paid no attention. "Who are you, and where are you taking
me?" she continued; but the giant said not a word. Close to

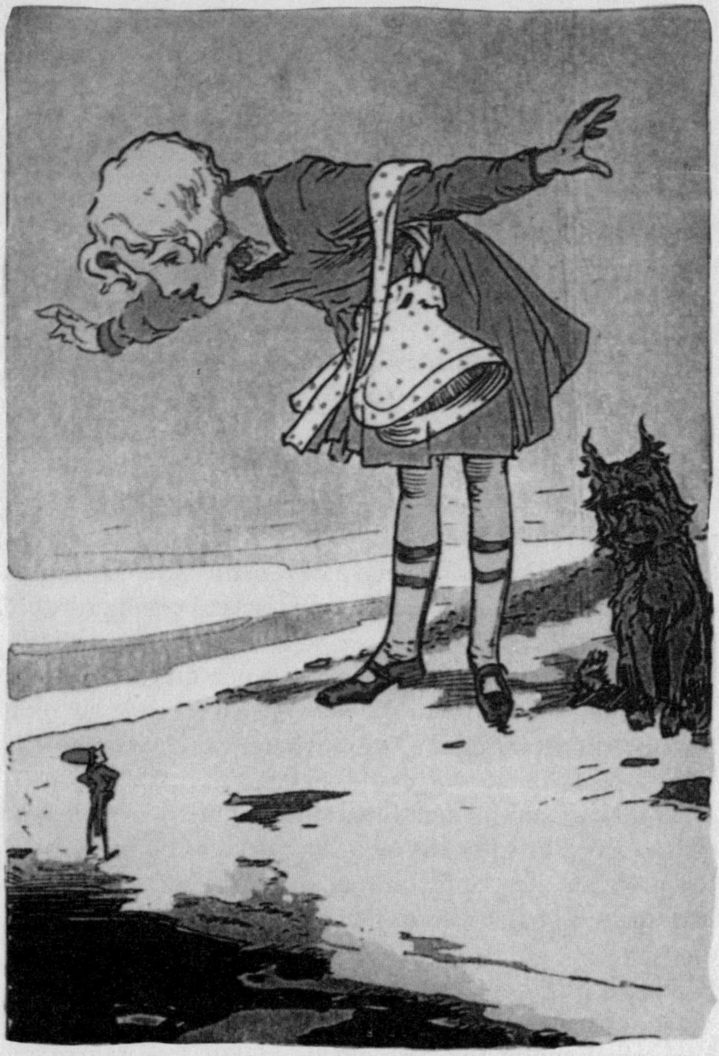

Dorothy's ear, however, a voice answered her, saying: "This is the terrible Crinklink, and he has you in his power."

Dorothy managed to twist her head around and found it was the second button on the jacket—the wolf's head—which had spoken to her.

"What will Crinklink do with me?" she asked anxiously.

"No one knows. You must wait and see," replied the wolf.

"Some of his captives he whips," squeaked the weasel's head.

"Some he transforms into bugs, and other things," growled the bear's head.

"Some he enchants, so that they become doorknobs," sighed the cat's head.

"Some he makes his slaves—even as we are—and that is the most dreadful fate of all," added the field-mouse. "As long as Crinklink exists we shall remain buttons, but as there are no more buttonholes on his jacket he will probably make you a slave."

Dorothy began to wish she had not met Crinklink. Meantime, the giant took such big steps that he soon reached the heart of the hills, where, perched upon the highest peak, stood a log castle. Before this castle he paused to set down Dorothy and Toto, for Crinklink was at present far too large to enter his own doorway. So he made himself grow smaller, until he was about the size of an ordinary man. Then he said to Dorothy, in stern, commanding tones:

"Enter, girl!"

Dorothy obeyed and entered the castle, with Toto at her heels. She found the place to be merely one big room. There was a table and chair of ordinary size near the center, and at one side a wee bed that seemed scarcely big enough

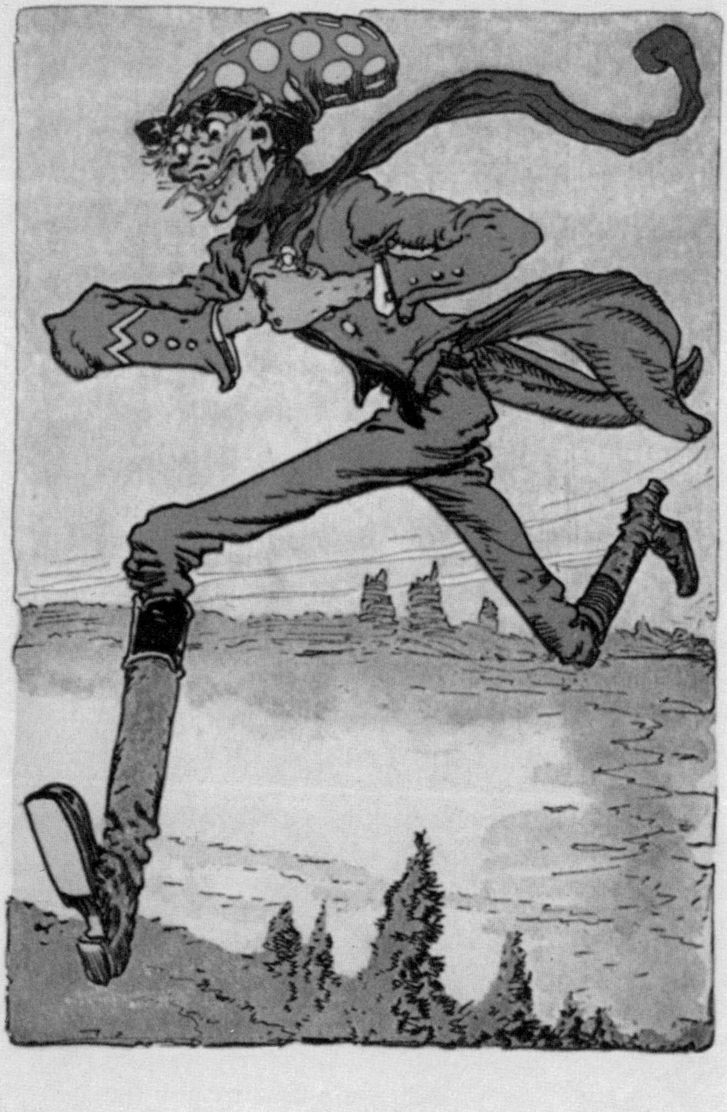

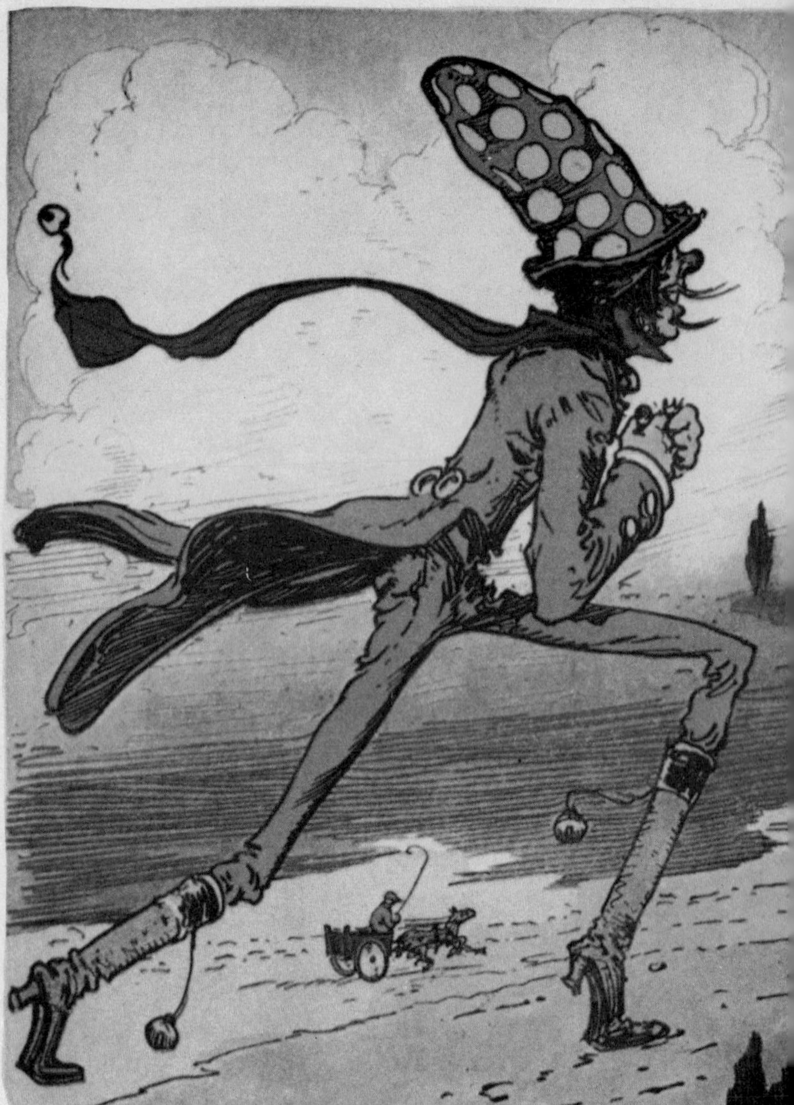

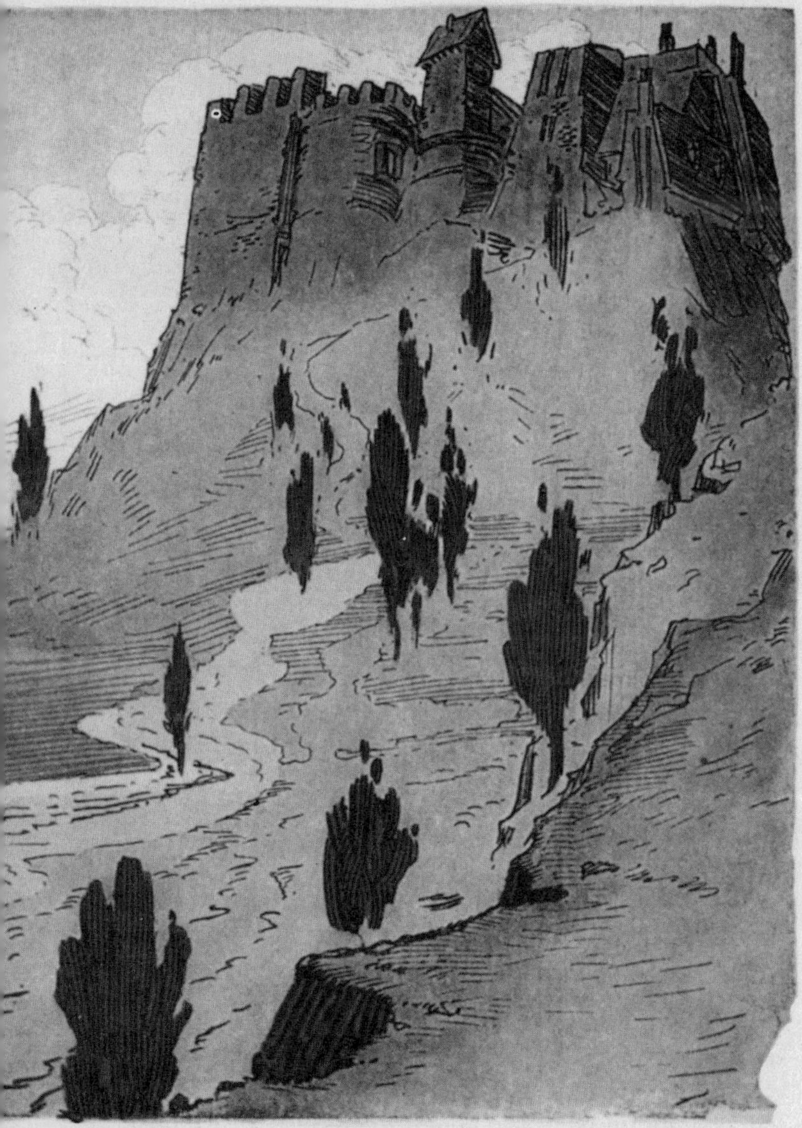

for a doll. Everywhere else were dishes—dishes—dishes! They were all soiled, and were piled upon the floor, in all the corners and upon every shelf. Evidently Crinklink hadn't washed a dish for years, but had cast them aside as he used them.

Dorothy's captor sat down in the chair and frowned at her.

"You are young and strong, and will make a good dish-washer," said he.

"Do you mean me to wash all those dishes?" she asked, feeling both indignant and fearful, for such a task would take weeks to accomplish.

"That's just what I mean," he retorted. "I need clean dishes, for all I have are soiled, and you're going to make 'em clean or get trounced. So get to work and be careful not to break anything. If you smash a dish, the penalty is one lash from my dreadful cat-o'-nine-tails for every piece the dish breaks into," and here Crinklink displayed a terrible whip that made the little girl shudder.

Dorothy knew how to wash dishes, but she remembered that often she carelessly broke one. In this case, however, a good deal depended on being careful, so she handled the dishes very cautiously.

While she worked, Toto sat by the hearth and growled low at Crinklink, and Crinklink sat in his chair and growled at Dorothy because she moved so slowly. He expected her to break a dish any minute, but as the hours passed away and this did not happen Crinklink began to grow sleepy. It was tiresome watching the girl wash dishes and often he began to yawn, and he yawned and yawned until finally he said:

"I'm going to take a nap. But the buttons on my jacket will be wide awake and whenever you break a dish the crash

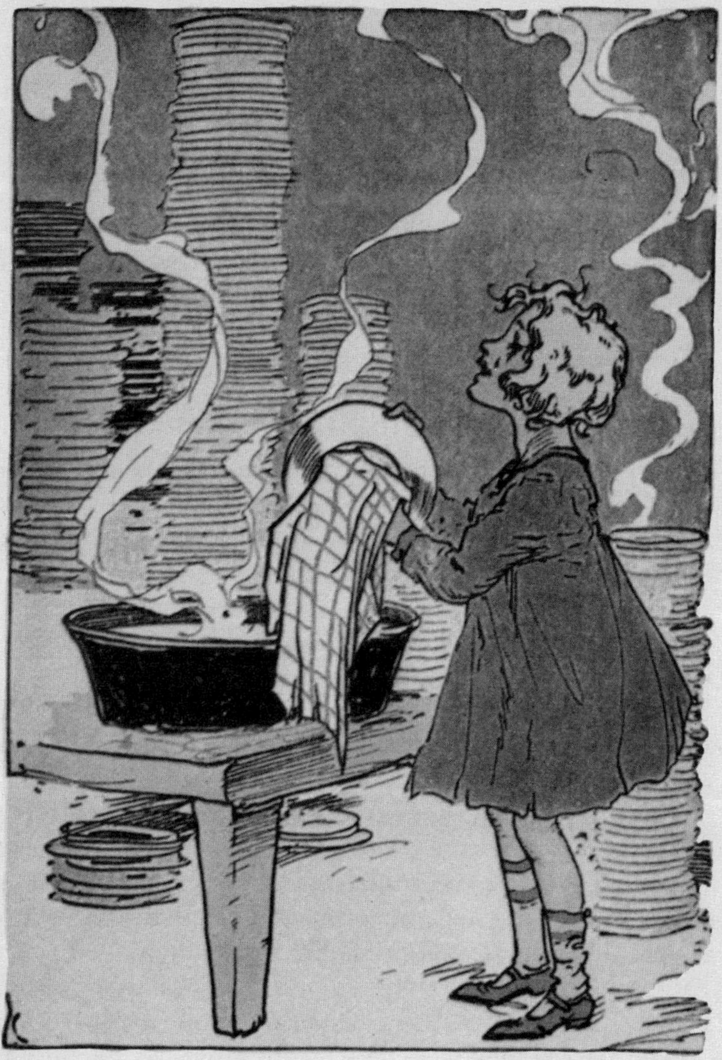

will waken me. As I'm rather sleepy, I hope you won't inter-
rupt my nap by breaking anything for a long time."

Then Crinklink made himself grow smaller and smaller
until he was three inches high and of a size to fit the tiny
bed. At once he lay down and fell fast asleep.

Dorothy came close to the buttons and whispered:
"Would you really warn Crinklink if I tried to escape?"

"You can't escape," growled the bear. "Crinklink would
become a giant, and soon overtake you."

"But you might kill him, while he sleeps," suggested the
cat, in a soft voice.

"Oh!" cried Dorothy, drawing back; "I couldn't poss'bly
kill anything—even to save my life."

But Toto had heard this conversation and was not so par-
ticular about killing monsters. Also the little dog knew he
must try to save his mistress. In an instant he sprang upon
the wee bed and was about to seize the sleeping Crinklink in
his jaws when Dorothy heard a loud crash and a heap of
dishes fell from the table to the floor. Then the girl saw Toto
and the little man rolling on the floor together, like a fuzzy
ball, and when the ball stopped rolling, behold! there sat
the little Wizard of Oz, laughing merrily at the expression
of surprise on Dorothy's face.

"Yes, my dear, it's me," said he, "and I've been playing
tricks on you—for your own good. I wanted to prove to you
that it is really dangerous for a little girl to wander alone in a
fairy country; so I took the form of Crinklink to teach you a
lesson. There isn't any Crinklink, to be sure; but if there
had been you'd be severely whipped for breaking all those
dishes."

The Wizard now rose, took off the coat with the button
heads, and spread it on the floor, wrong side up. At once
there crept from beneath it a bear, a wolf, a cat, a weasel, and

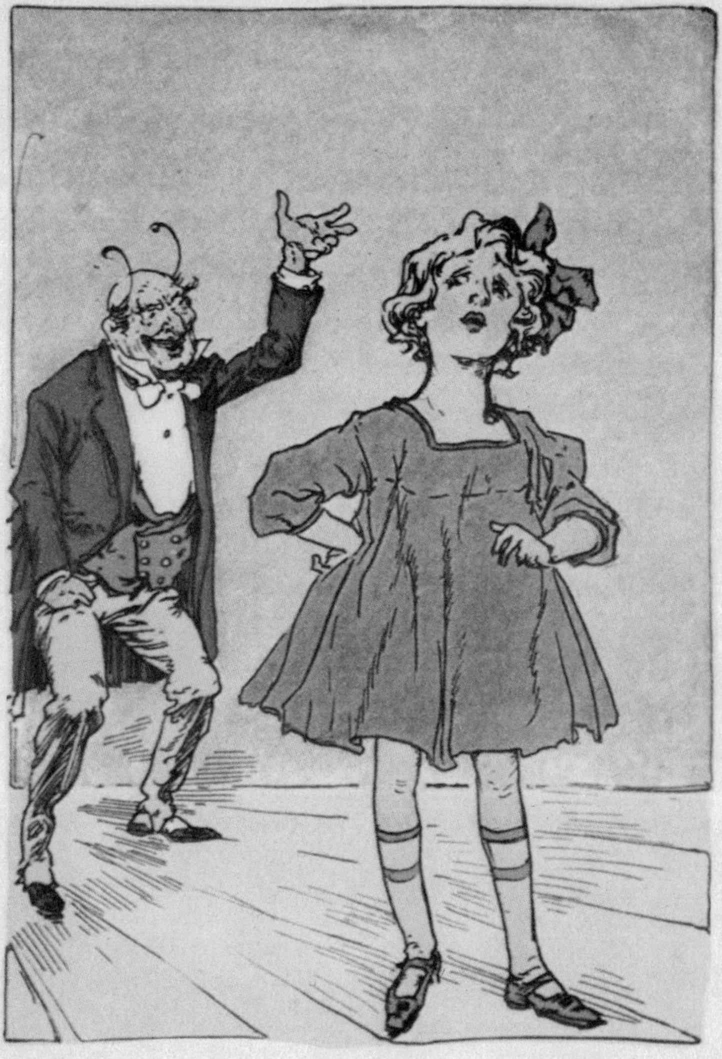

a field-mouse, who all rushed from the room and escaped into the mountains.

"Come on, Toto," said Dorothy; "let's go back to the Emerald City. You've given me a good scare, Wizard," she added, with dignity, "and p'raps I'll forgive you, by'n'by; but just now I'm mad to think how easily you fooled me."

TIK-TOK
and
THE NOME KING

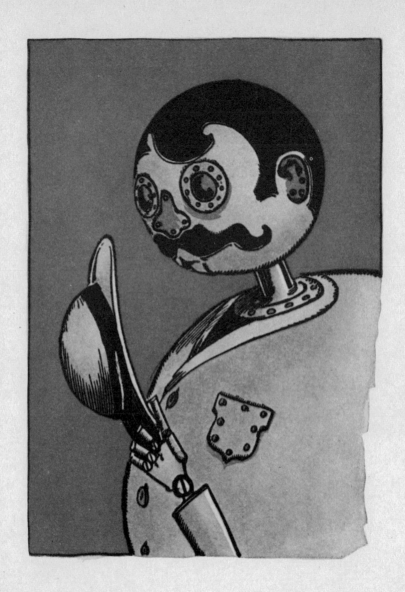

TIK-TOK AND THE NOME KING

 THE Nome King was unpleasantly angry. He had carelessly bitten his tongue at breakfast and it still hurt; so he roared and raved and stamped around in his underground palace in a way that rendered him very disagreeable.

It so happened that on this unfortunate day Tik-Tok, the Clockwork Man, visited the Nome King to ask a favor. Tik-Tok lived in the Land of Oz and although he was an active and important person, he was made entirely of metal. Machinery within him, something like the works of a clock, made him move; other machinery made him talk; still other machinery made him think.

Although so cleverly constructed, the Clockwork Man was far from perfect. Three separate keys wound up his motion machinery, his speech works, and his thoughts. One or more of these contrivances was likely to run down at a critical moment, leaving poor Tik-Tok helpless. Also some of his parts were wearing out, through much use, and just now his thought machinery needed repair. The skillful little Wizard of Oz had tinkered with Tik-Tok's thoughts without being able to get them properly regulated, so he had advised the Clockwork Man to go to the Nome King and secure a new set of springs, which would render his thoughts more elastic and responsive.

"Be careful what you say to the Nome King," warned the Wizard. "He has a bad temper and the least little thing makes him angry."

Tik-Tok promised, and the Wizard wound his machinery and set him walking in the direction of the Nome King's dominions, just across the desert from the Land of Oz. He ran down just as he reached the entrance to the underground palace, and there Kaliko, the Nome King's Chief Steward, found him and wound him up again.

"I want to see the King," said Tik-Tok, in his jerky voice.

"Well," remarked Kaliko, "it may be safe for a cast-iron person like you to face his Majesty this morning; but you must announce yourself, for should I show my face inside the jewel-studded cavern where the King is now raving, I'd soon look like a dish of mashed potatoes, and be of no further use to anyone."

"I'm not a-fraid," said Tik-Tok.

"Then walk in and make yourself at home," answered Kaliko, and threw open the door of the King's cavern.

Tik-Tok promptly walked in and faced the astonished Nome King, to whom he said: "Good morn-ing. I want two new steel springs for my thought-works and a new cog-wheel for my speech-pro-du-cer. How a-bout it, your Maj-es-ty?"

The Nome King growled a menacing growl and his eyes were red with rage.

"How dare you enter my presence?" he shouted.

"I dare an-y-thing," said Tik-Tok. "I'm not a-fraid of a fat Nome."

This was true, yet an unwise speech. Had Tik-Tok's thoughts been in good working order he would have said

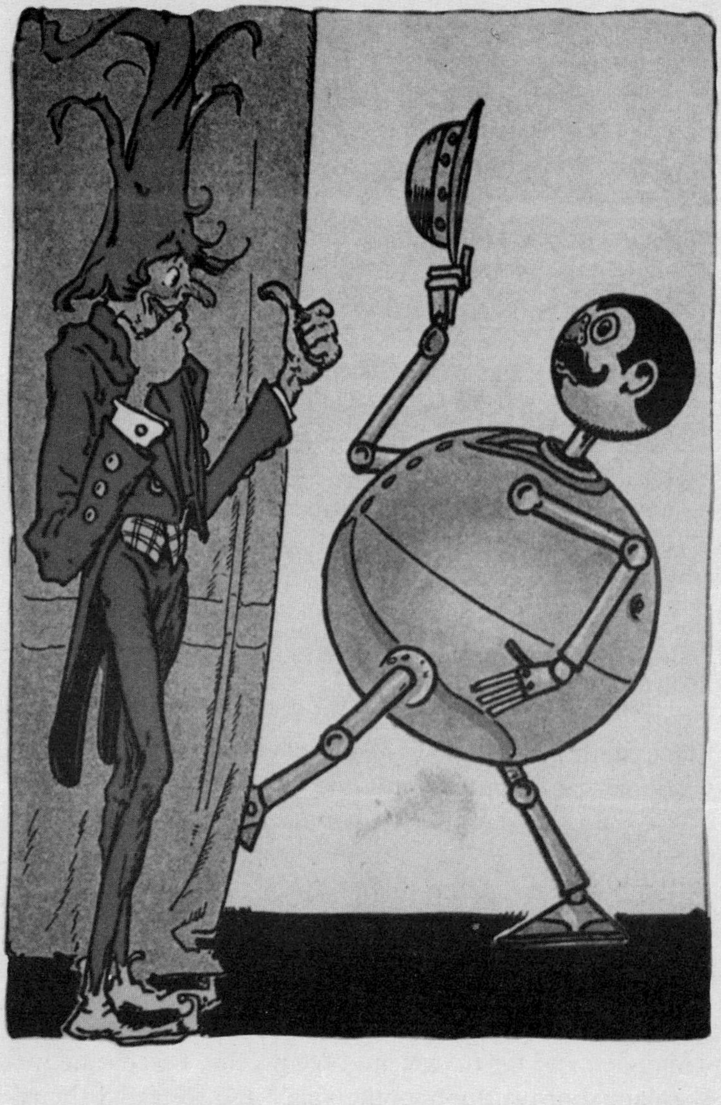

something else. The angry Nome King quickly caught up his heavy mace and hurled it straight at Tik-Tok. When it struck the metal man's breast, the force of the blow burst the bolts which held the plates of his body together and they clattered to the floor in a score of pieces. Hundreds and hundreds of wheels, pins, cogs, and springs filled the air like a cloud and then rattled like hail upon the floor.

Where Tik-Tok had stood was now only a scrap-heap and the Nome King was so amazed by the terrible effect of his blow that he stared in wonder.

His Majesty's anger quickly cooled. He remembered that the Clockwork Man was a favorite subject of the powerful Princess, Ozma of Oz, who would be sure to resent Tik-Tok's ruin.

"Too bad! Too bad!" he muttered, regretfully. "I'm really sorry I made junk of the fellow. I didn't know he'd break."

"You'd better be," remarked Kaliko, who now ventured to enter the room. "You'll have a war on your hands when Ozma hears of this, and the chances are you will lose your throne and your kingdom."

The Nome King turned pale, for he loved to rule the Nomes and did not know of any other way to earn a living in case Ozma fought and conquered him.

"Do—do you think Ozma will be angry?" he asked anxiously.

"I'm sure of it," said Kaliko. "And she has the right to be. You've made scrap-iron of her favorite."

The King groaned.

"Sweep him up and throw the rubbish into the black pit," he commanded; and then he shut himself up in his private den and for days would see no one, because he was so ashamed of his unreasoning anger and so feared the results of his rash act.

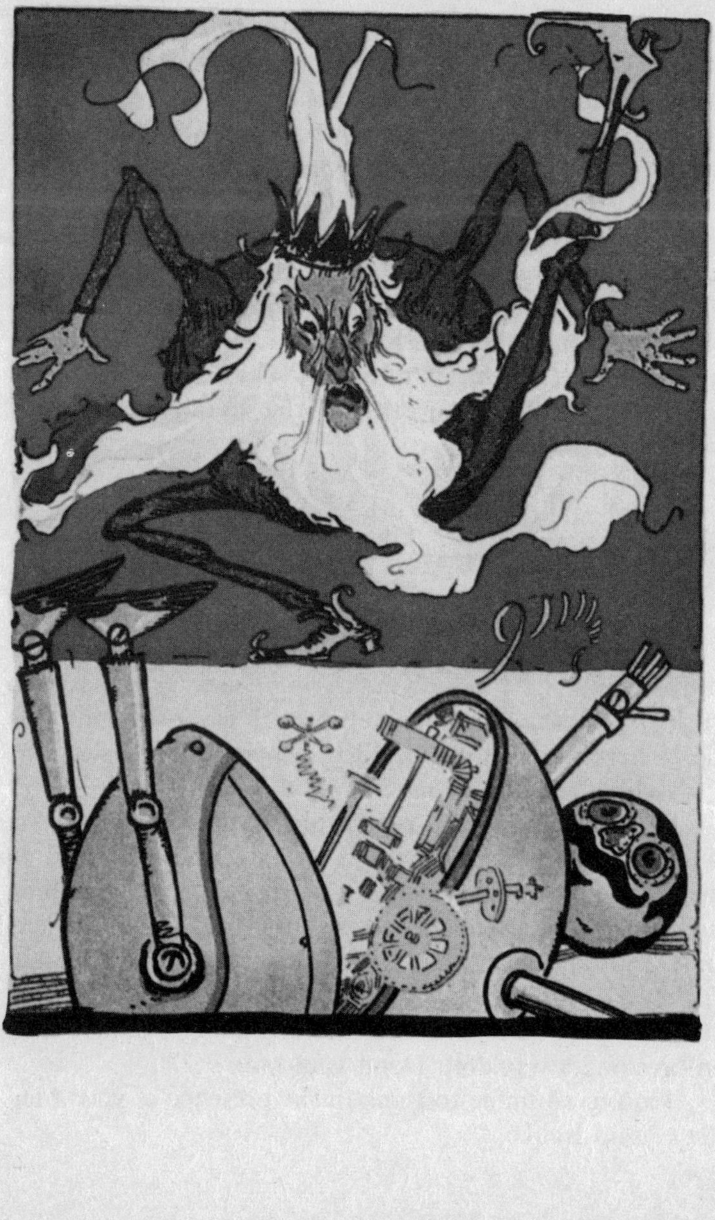

Kaliko swept up the pieces, but he did not throw them into the black pit. Being a clever and skillful mechanic he determined to fit the pieces together again.

No man ever faced a greater puzzle; but it was interesting work and Kaliko succeeded. When he found a spring or wheel worn or imperfect, he made a new one. Within two weeks, by working steadily night and day, the Chief Steward completed his task and put the three sets of clockworks and the last rivet into Tik-Tok's body. He then wound up the motion machinery and the Clockwork Man walked up and down the room as naturally as ever. Then Kaliko wound up the thought works and the speech regulator and said to Tik-Tok:

"How do you feel now?"

"Fine," said the Clockwork Man. "You have done a ve-ry good job, Kal-i-ko, and saved me from de-struc-tion. Much o-bliged."

"Don't mention it," replied the Chief Steward. "I quite enjoyed the work."

Just then the Nome King's gong sounded and Kaliko rushed away through the jewel-studded cavern and into the den where the King had hidden, leaving the doors ajar.

"Kaliko," said the King, in a meek voice, "I've been shut up here long enough to repent bitterly the destruction of Tik-Tok. Of course Ozma will have revenge, and send an army to fight us, but we must take our medicine. One thing comforts me: Tik-Tok wasn't really a live person; he was only a machine man, and so it wasn't very wicked to stop his clockworks. I couldn't sleep nights, at first, for worry; but there's no more harm in smashing a machine man than in breaking a wax doll. Don't you think so?"

"I am too humble to think in the presence of your Majesty," said Kaliko.

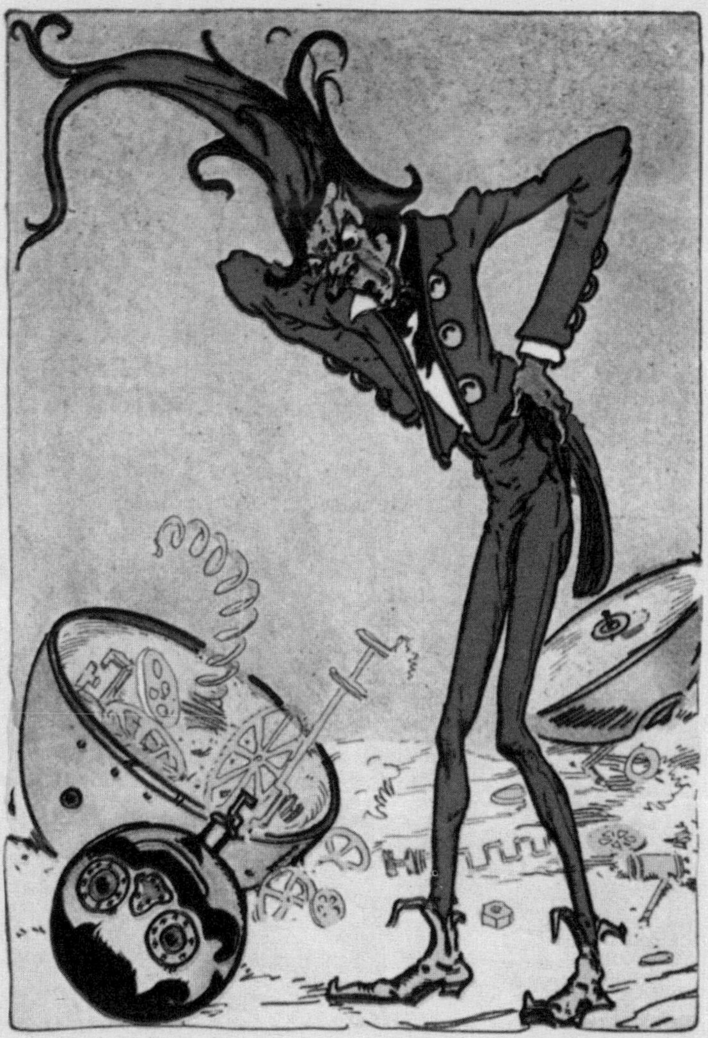

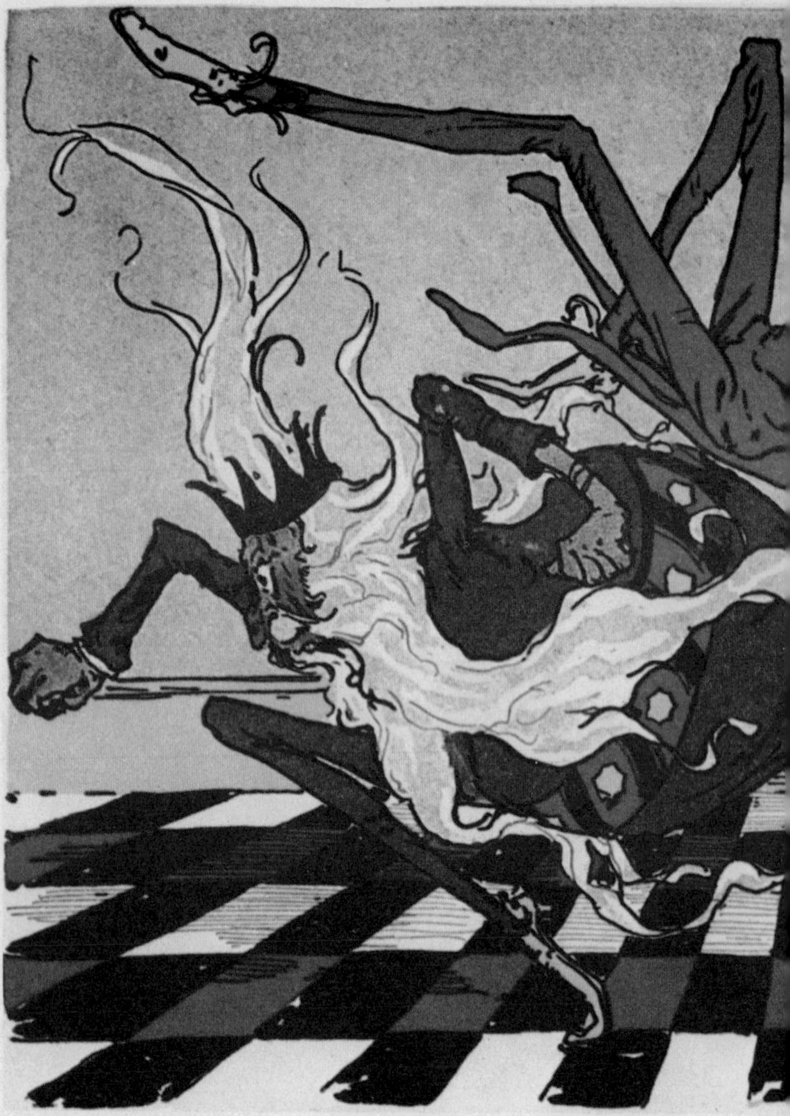

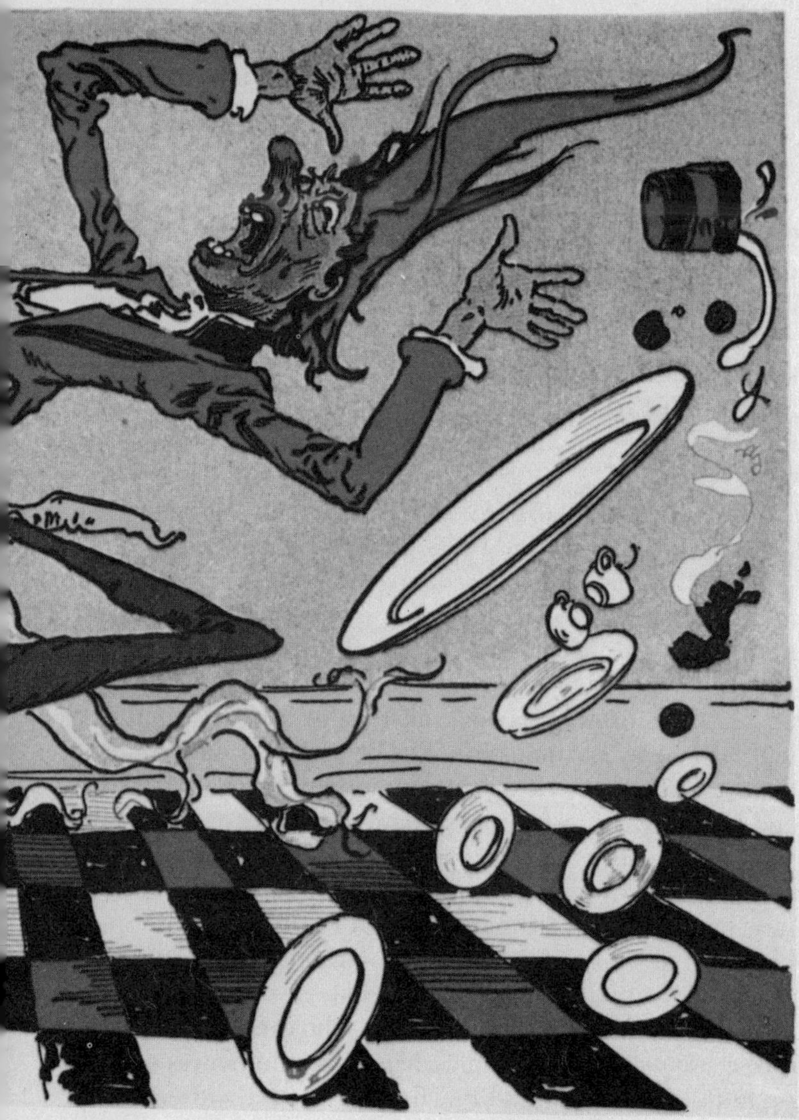

"Then get me something to eat," commanded the King, "for I'm nearly starved. Two roasted goats, a barrel of cakes, and nine mince pies will do me until dinnertime."

Kaliko bowed and hurried away to the royal kitchen, forgetting Tik-Tok, who was wandering around in the outer cavern. Suddenly the Nome King looked up and saw the Clockwork Man standing before him, and at the sight the monarch's eyes grew big and round and he fell a-trembling in every limb.

"Away, grim Shadow!" he cried. "You're not here, you know; you're only a hash of cogwheels and springs, lying at the bottom of the black pit. Vanish, thou Vision of the demolished Tik-Tok, and leave me in peace—for I have bitterly repented!"

"Then beg my par-don," said Tik-Tok in a gruff voice, for Kaliko had forgotten to oil the speech works.

But the sound of a voice coming from what he thought a mere vision was too much for the Nome King's shaken nerves. He gave a yell of fear and rushed from the room. Tik-Tok followed, as the King bolted through the corridors on a swift run and bumped against Kaliko, who was returning with a tray of things to eat. The sound of the breaking dishes, as they struck the floor, added to the King's terror and he yelled again and dashed into a great cavern where a thousand Nomes were at work hammering metal.

"Look out! Here comes a phantom clockwork man!" screamed the terrified monarch, and every Nome dropped his tools and made a rush from the cavern, knocking over their King in their mad flight and recklessly trampling upon his prostrate fat body. So, when Tik-Tok came into the cavern, there was only the Nome King left, and he was rolling upon the rocky floor and howling for mercy, with his eyes

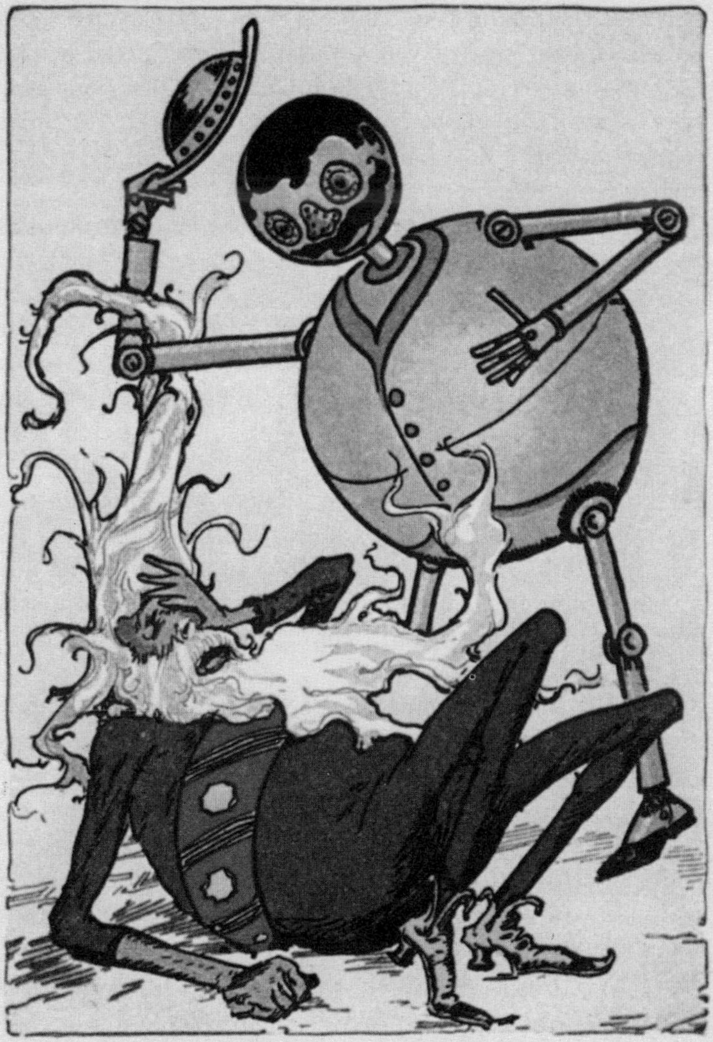

fast shut so that he could not see what he was sure was a dreadful phantom that was coming straight toward him.

"It oc-curs to me," said Tik-Tok calmly, "that your Maj-es-ty is act-ing like a ba-by. I am not a phan-tom. A phan-tom is un-real, while I am the real thing."

The King rolled over, sat up and opened his eyes.

"Didn't I smash you to pieces?" he asked in trembling tones.

"Yes," said Tik-Tok.

"Then you are nothing but a junk-heap, and this form in which you now appear cannot be real."

"It is, though," declared Tik-Tok. "Kal-i-ko picked up my piec-es and put me to-geth-er a-gain. I'm as good as new, and per-haps bet-ter."

"That is true, your Majesty," added Kaliko, who now made his appearance, "and I hope you will forgive me for mending Tik-Tok. He was quite broken up, after you smashed him, and I found it almost as hard a job to match his pieces as to pick turnips from gooseberry bushes. But I did it," he added proudly.

"You are forgiven," announced the Nome King, rising to his feet and drawing a long breath. "I will raise your wages one specto a year, and Tik-Tok shall return to the Land of Oz loaded with jewels for the Princess Ozma."

"That is all right," said Tik-Tok. "But what I want to know is, why did you hit me with your mace?"

"Because I was angry," admitted the King. "When I am angry, I always do something that I am sorry for afterward. So I have firmly resolved never to get angry again; unless—unless—"

"Unless what, your Majesty?" inquired Kaliko.

"Unless something annoys me," said the Nome King. And then he went to his treasure-chamber to get the jewels for Princess Ozma of Oz.

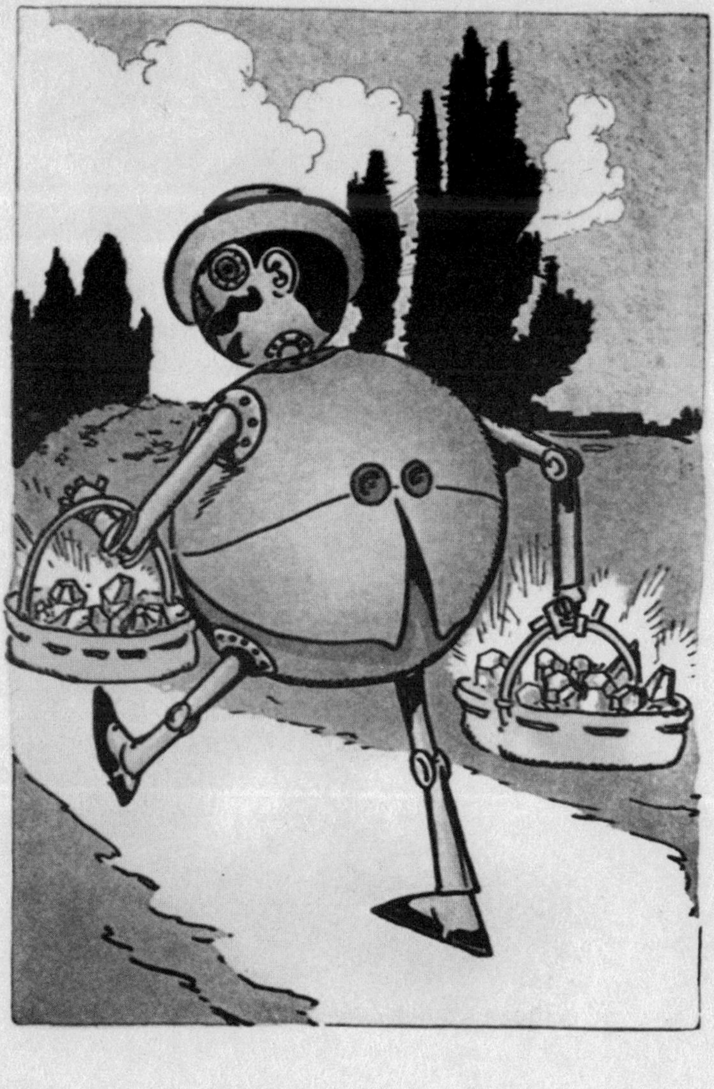

OZMA

and

THE LITTLE WIZARD

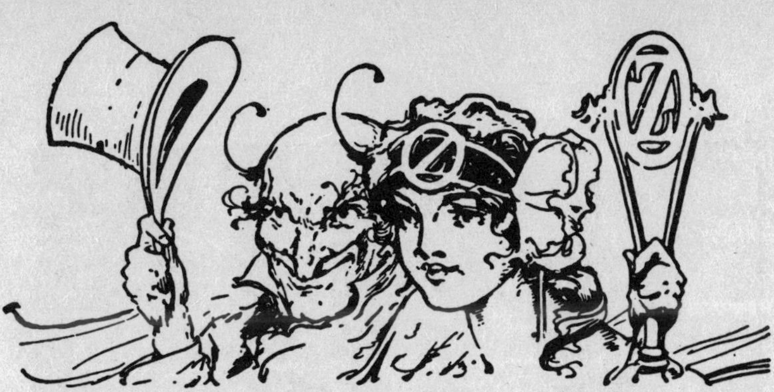

OZMA AND THE LITTLE WIZARD

ONCE upon a time there lived in the beautiful Emerald City, which lies in the center of the fairy Land of Oz, a lovely girl called Princess Ozma, who was Ruler of all that country. And among those who served this girlish Ruler and lived in a cozy suite of rooms in her splendid palace, was a little, withered old man known as the Wizard of Oz.

This little Wizard could do a good many queer things in magic; but he was a kind man, with merry, twinkling eyes and a sweet smile; so, instead of fearing him because of his magic, everybody loved him.

Now, Ozma was very anxious that all her people who inhabited the pleasant Land of Oz should be happy and contented, and therefore she decided one morning to make a journey to all parts of the country, that she might discover if anything was amiss, or anyone discontented, or if there was any wrong that ought to be righted. She asked the little Wizard to accompany her and he was glad to go.

"Shall I take my bag of magic tools with me?" he asked.

"Of course," said Ozma. "We may need a lot of magic before we return, for we are going into strange corners of

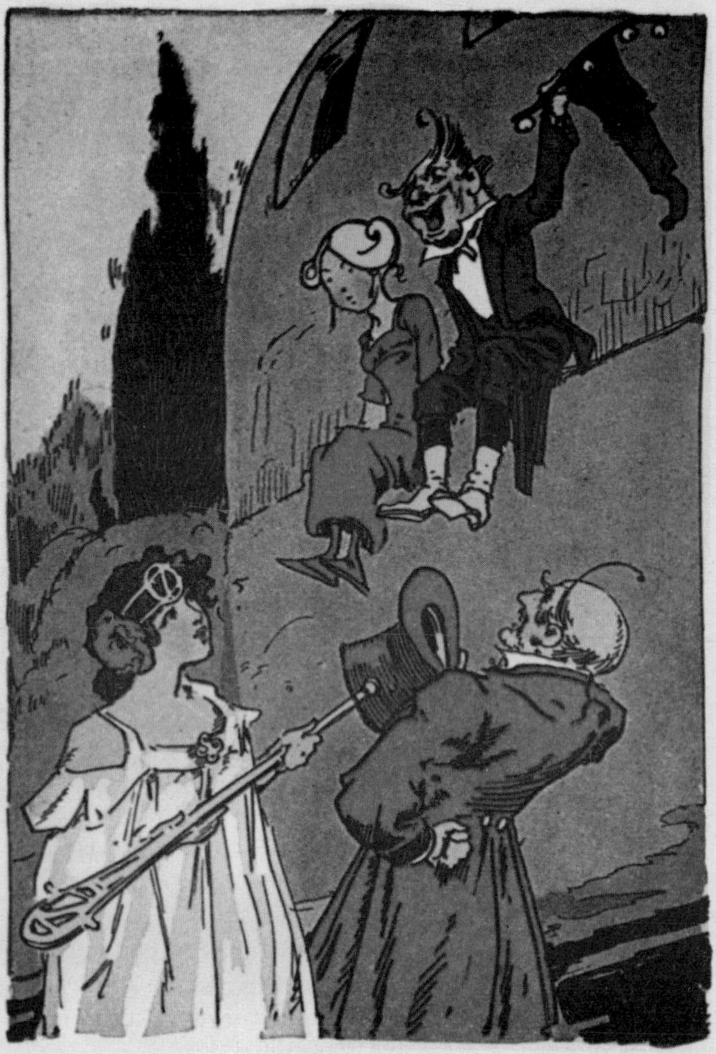

the land, where we may meet with unknown creatures and dangerous adventures."

So the Wizard took his bag of magic tools and the two left the Emerald City and wandered over the country for many days, at last reaching a place far up in the mountains which neither of them had ever visited before. Stopping one morning at a cottage, built beside the rocky path which led into a pretty valley beyond, Ozma asked a man:

"Are you happy? Have you any complaint to make of your lot?"

And the man replied:

"We are happy except for three mischievous Imps that live in yonder valley and often come here to annoy us. If your Highness would only drive away those Imps, I and my family would be very happy and very grateful to you."

"Who are these bad Imps?" inquired the girl Ruler.

"One is named Olite, and one Udent and one Ertinent, and they have no respect for anyone or anything. If strangers pass through the valley the Imps jeer at them and make horrid faces and call names, and often they push travelers out of the path or throw stones at them. Whenever Imp Olite or Imp Udent or Imp Ertinent comes here to bother us, I and my family run into the house and lock all the doors and windows, and we dare not venture out again until the Imps have gone away."

Princess Ozma was grieved to hear this report and the little Wizard shook his head gravely and said the naughty Imps deserved to be punished. They told the good man they would see what could be done to protect him and at once entered the valley to seek the dwelling place of the three mischievous creatures.

Before long they came upon three caves, hollowed from the rocks, and in front of each cave squatted a queer little

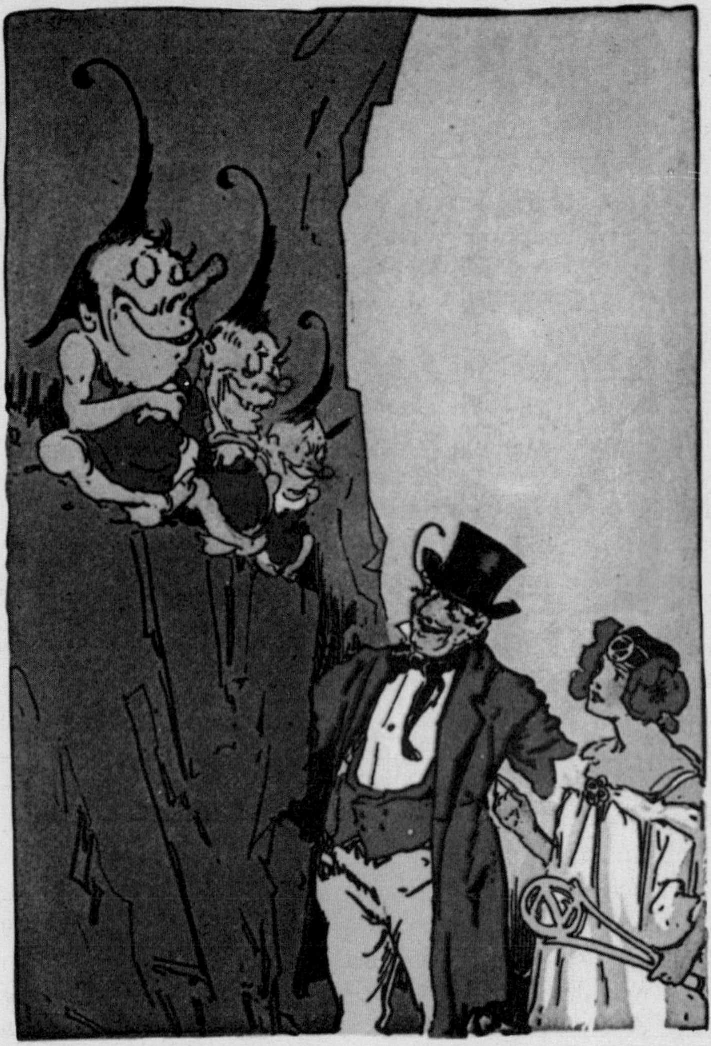

dwarf. Ozma and the Wizard paused to examine them and found them well-shaped, strong, and lively. They had big round ears, flat noses and wide, grinning mouths, and their jet-black hair came to points on top of their heads, much resembling horns. Their clothing fitted snugly to their bodies and limbs and the Imps were so small in size that at first Ozma did not consider them at all dangerous. But one of them suddenly reached out a hand and caught the dress of the Princess, jerking it so sharply that she nearly fell down, and a moment later another Imp pushed the little Wizard so hard that he bumped against Ozma and both un-expectedly sat down upon the ground.

At this the Imps laughed boisterously and began running around in a circle and kicking dust upon the Royal Princess, who cried in a sharp voice: "Wizard, do your duty!"

The Wizard promptly obeyed. Without rising from the ground he opened his bag, got the tools he required and muttered a magic spell.

Instantly the three Imps became three bushes—of a thorny, stubby kind—with their roots in the ground. As the bushes were at first motionless, perhaps through surprise at their sudden transformation, the Wizard and the Princess found time to rise from the ground and brush the dust off their pretty clothes. Then Ozma turned to the bushes and said:

"The unhappy lot you now endure, my poor Imps, is due entirely to your naughty actions. You can no longer annoy harmless travelers and you must remain ugly bushes, cov-ered with sharp thorns, until you repent of your bad ways and promise to be good Imps."

"They can't help being good, now, your Highness," said the Wizard, who was much pleased with his work, "and the safest plan will be to allow them always to remain bushes."

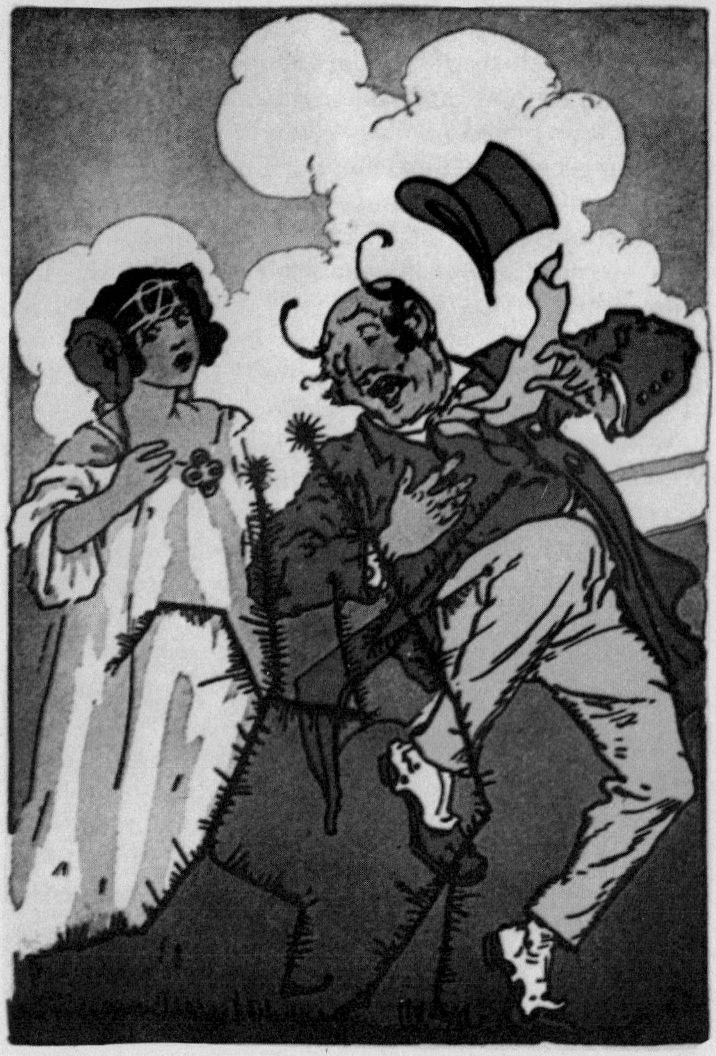

But something must have been wrong with the Wizard's magic, or the creatures had magic of their own, for no sooner were the words spoken than the bushes began to move. At first they only waved their branches at the girl and the little man, but pretty soon they began to slide over the ground, their roots dragging through the earth, and one pushed itself against the Wizard and pricked him so sharply with its thorns that he cried out: "Ouch!" and started to run away.

Ozma followed, for the other bushes were trying to stick their thorns into her legs and one actually got so near her that it tore a great rent in her beautiful dress. The girl Princess could run, however, and she followed the fleeing Wizard until he tumbled head first over a log and rolled upon the ground. Then she sprang behind a tree and shouted: "Quick! Transform them into something else."

The Wizard heard, but he was much confused by his fall. Grabbing from his bag the first magical tool he could find he transformed the bushes into three white pigs. That astonished the Imps. In the shape of pigs—fat, roly-poly and cute—they scampered off a little distance and sat down to think about their new condition.

Ozma drew a long breath and coming from behind the tree she said:

"That is much better, Wiz, for such pigs as these must be quite harmless. No one need now fear the mischievous Imps."

"I intended to transform them into mice," replied the Wizard, "but in my excitement I worked the wrong magic. However, unless the horrid creatures behave themselves hereafter, they are liable to be killed and eaten. They would make good chops, sausages, or roasts."

But the Imps were now angry and had no intention of

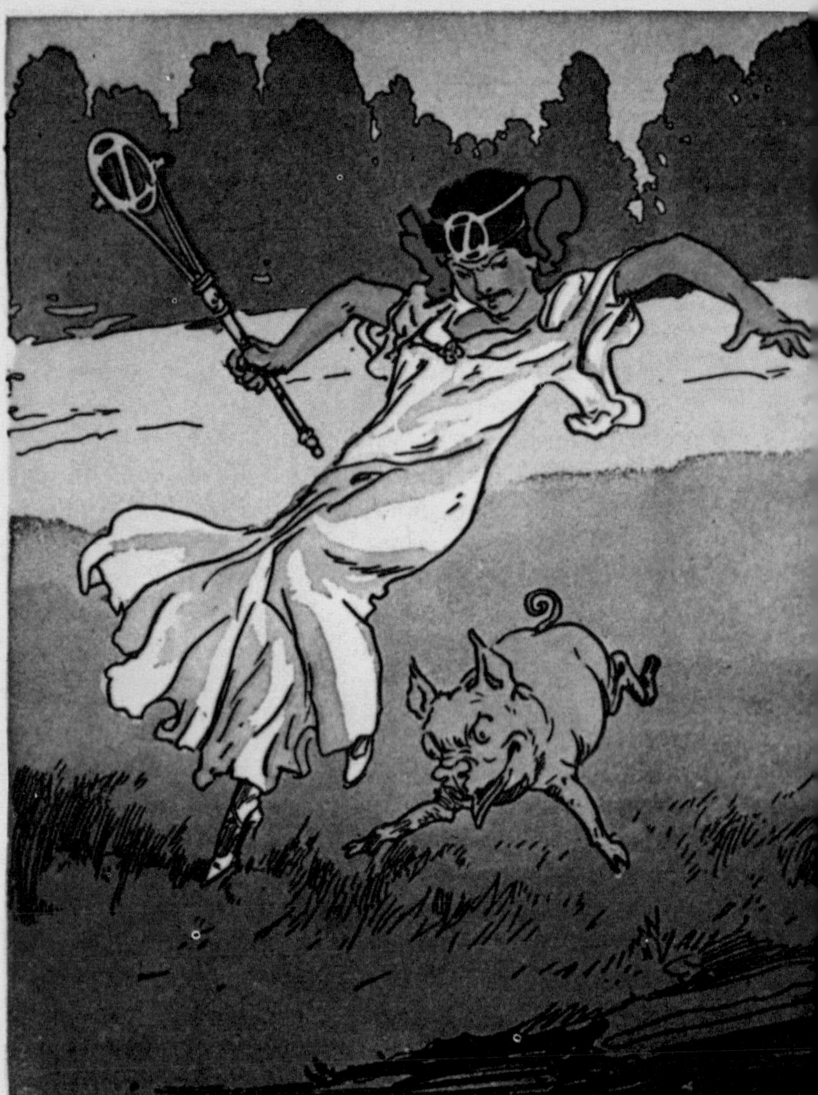

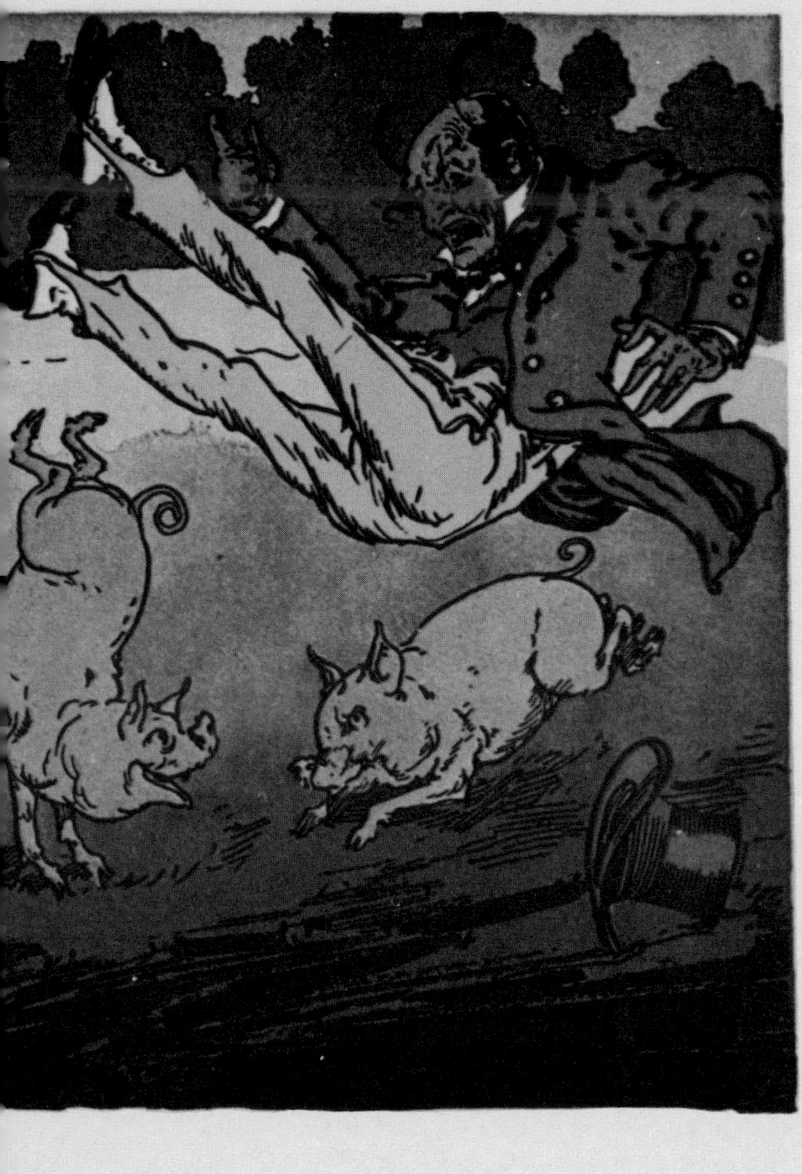

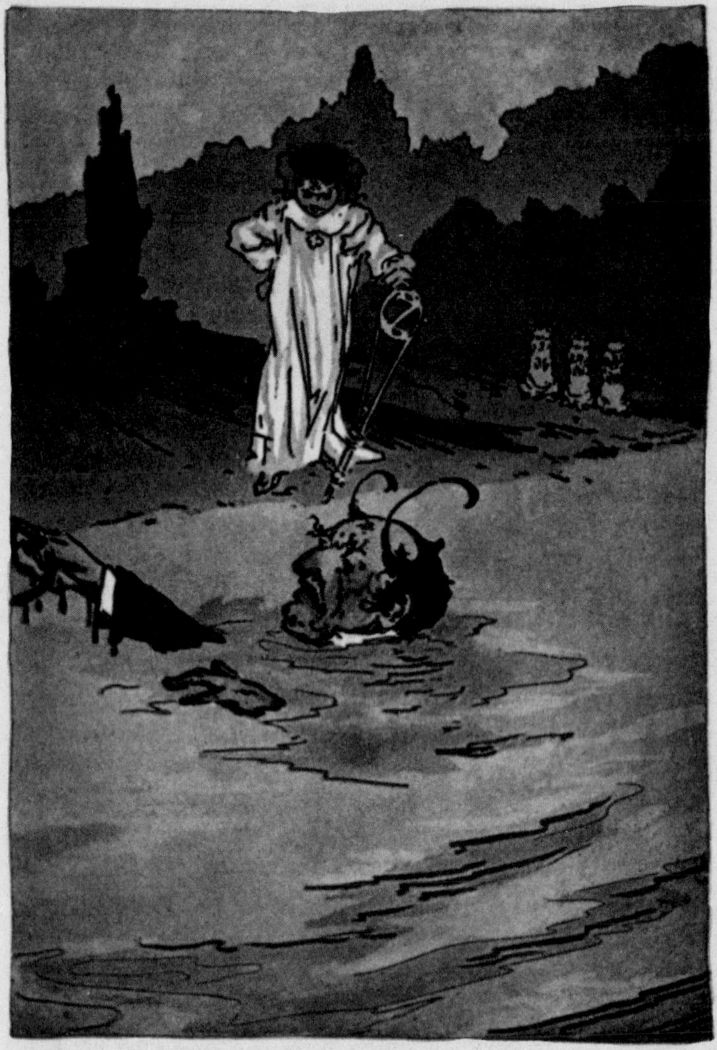

behaving. As Ozma and the little Wizard turned to resume their journey the three pigs rushed forward, dashed between their legs, and tripped them up, so that both lost their balance and toppled over, clinging to one another. As the Wizard tried to get up he was tripped again and fell across the back of the third pig, which carried him on a run far down the valley until it dumped the little man into the river. Ozma had been sprawled upon the ground but found she was not hurt, so she picked herself up and ran to the assistance of the Wizard, reaching him just as he was crawling out of the river, gasping for breath and dripping with water. The girl could not help laughing at his woeful appearance. But he had no sooner wiped the wet from his eyes than one of the impish pigs tripped him again and sent him into the river for a second bath. The pigs tried to trip Ozma, too, but she ran around a stump and so managed to keep out of their way. So the Wizard scrambled out of the water again and picked up a sharp stick to defend himself. Then he mumbled a magic mutter which instantly dried his clothes, after which he hurried to assist Ozma. The pigs were afraid of the sharp stick and kept away from it.

"This won't do," said the Princess. "We have accomplished nothing, for the pig Imps would annoy travelers as much as the real Imps. Transform them into something else, Wiz."

The Wizard took time to think. Then he transformed the white pigs into three blue doves.

"Doves," said he, "are the most harmless things in the world."

But scarcely had he spoken when the doves flew at them and tried to peck out their eyes. When they endeavored to shield their eyes with their hands two of the doves bit the Wizard's fingers and another caught the pretty pink ear of

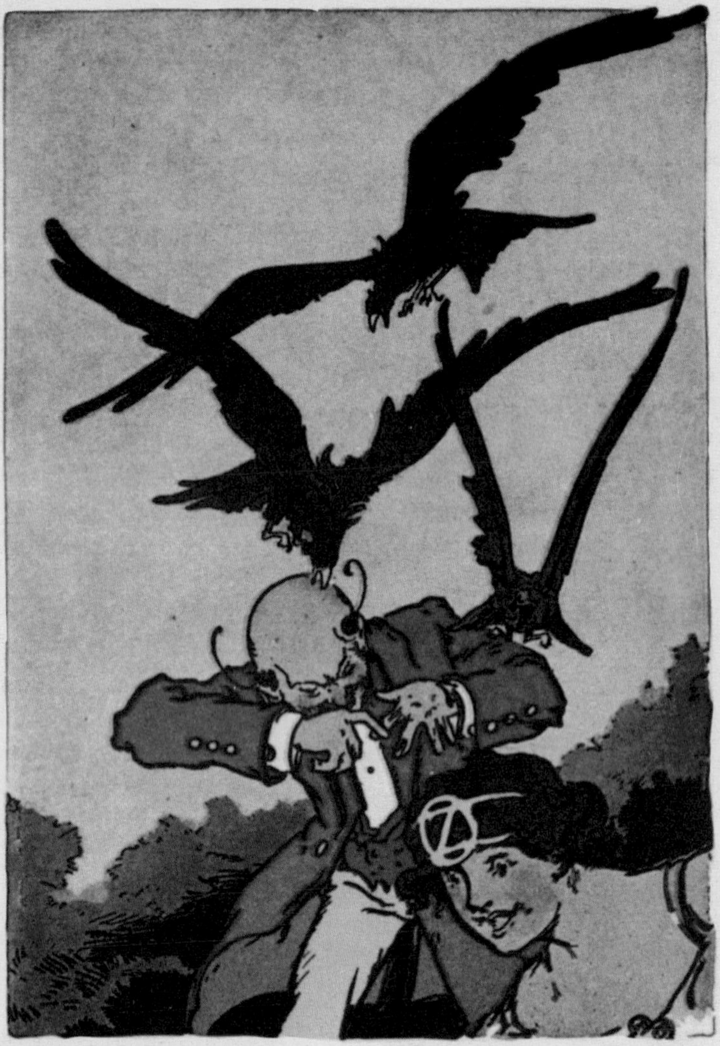

the Princess in its bill and gave it such a cruel tweak that she cried out in pain and threw her skirt over her head.

"These birds are worse than the pigs, Wizard," she called to her companion. "Nothing is harmless that is animated by impudent anger or impertinent mischief. You must transform the Imps into something that is not alive."

The Wizard was pretty busy, just then, driving off the birds, but he managed to open his bag of magic and find a charm which instantly transformed the doves into three buttons. As they fell to the ground he picked them up and smiled with satisfaction. The tin button was Imp Olite, the brass button was Imp Udent and the lead button was Imp Ertinent. These buttons the Wizard placed in a little box which he put in his jacket pocket.

"Now," said he, "the Imps cannot annoy travelers, for we shall carry them back with us to the Emerald City."

"But we dare not use the buttons," said Ozma, smiling once more now that the danger was over.

"Why not?" asked the Wizard. "I intend to sew them upon my coat and watch them carefully. The spirits of the Imps are still in the buttons, and after a time they will repent and be sorry for their naughtiness. Then they will decide to be very good in the future. When they feel that way, the tin button will turn to silver and the brass to gold, while the lead button will become aluminum. I shall then restore them to their proper forms, changing their names to pretty names instead of the ugly ones they used to bear. Thereafter the three Imps will become good citizens of the Land of Oz, and I think you will find they will prove faithful subjects of our beloved Princess Ozma."

"Ah, that is magic well worth while," exclaimed Ozma, well pleased. "There is no doubt, my friend, but that you are a very clever Wizard."

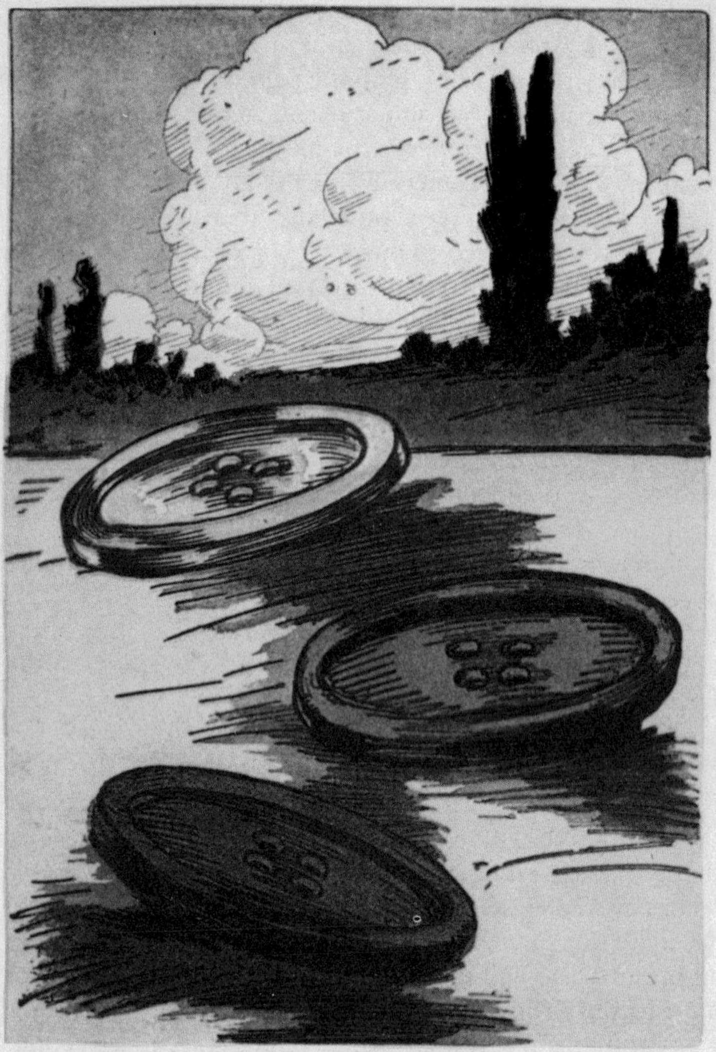

Jack Pumpkinhead
and
The Sawhorse

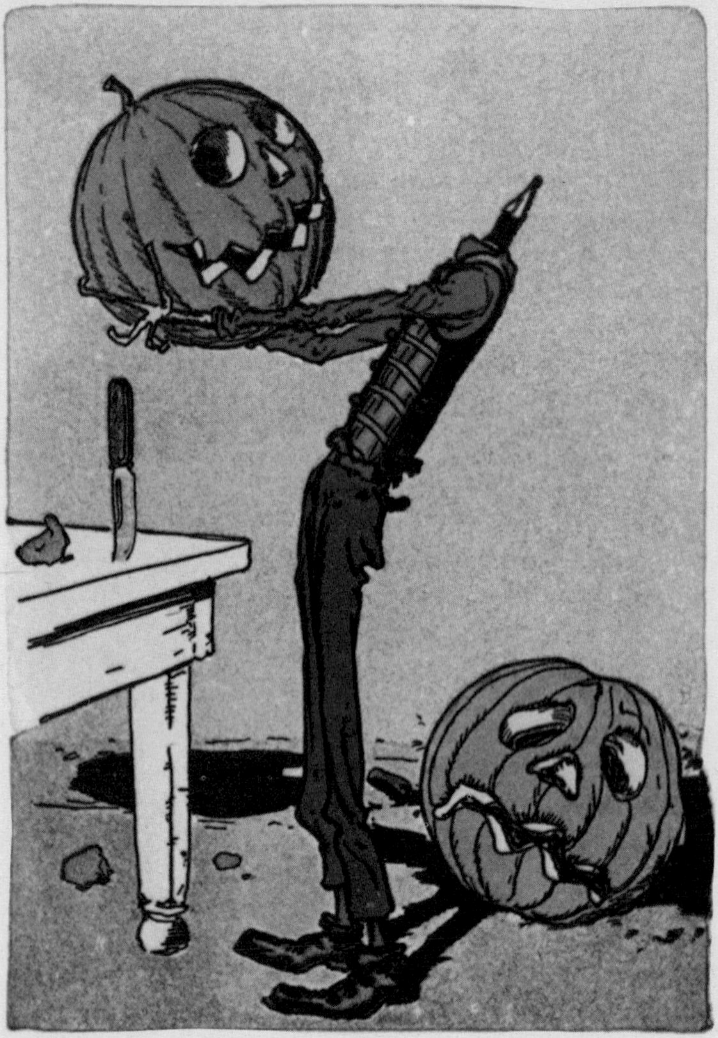

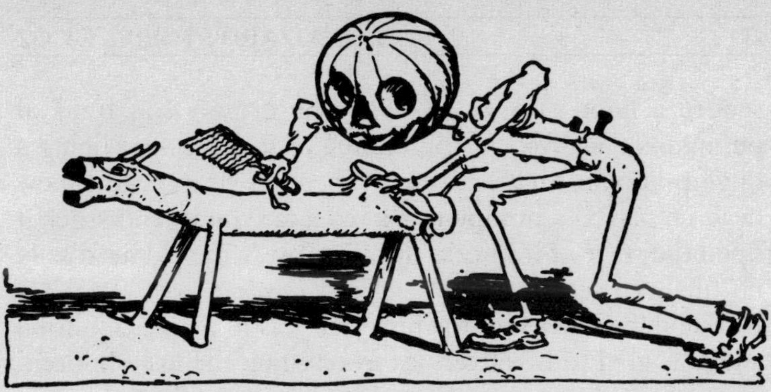

JACK PUMPKINHEAD AND THE SAWHORSE

IN a room of the Royal Palace of the Emerald City of Oz hangs a Magic Picture, in which are shown all the important scenes that transpire in those fairy dominions. The scenes shift constantly, and by watching them, Ozma, the girl Ruler, is able to discover events taking place in any part of her kingdom.

One day she saw in her Magic Picture that a little girl and a little boy had wandered together into a great, gloomy forest at the far west of Oz and had become hopelessly lost. Their friends were seeking them in the wrong direction and unless Ozma came to their rescue the little ones would never be found in time to save them from starving.

So the Princess sent a message to Jack Pumpkinhead and asked him to come to the palace. This personage, one of the queerest of the queer inhabitants of Oz, was an old friend and companion of Ozma. His form was made of rough sticks fitted together and dressed in ordinary clothes. His head was a pumpkin with a face carved upon it, and was set on top a sharp stake which formed his neck.

Jack was active, good-natured and a general favorite; but his pumpkin head was likely to spoil with age, so in order to secure a good supply of heads he grew a big field of pumpkins and lived in the middle of it, his house being a huge pumpkin hollowed out. Whenever he needed a new head he picked a pumpkin, carved a face on it, and stuck it upon the stake of his neck, throwing away the old head as of no further use.

The day Ozma sent for him Jack was in prime condition and was glad to be of service in rescuing the lost children. Ozma made him a map, showing just where the forest was and how to get to it and the paths he must take to reach the little ones. Then she said:

"You'd better ride the Sawhorse, for he is swift and intelligent and will help you accomplish your task."

"All right," answered Jack, and went to the royal stable to tell the Sawhorse to be ready for the trip.

This remarkable animal was not unlike Jack Pumpkinhead in form, although so different in shape. Its body was a log, with four sticks stuck into it for legs. A branch at one end of the log served as a tail, while in the other end was chopped a gash that formed a mouth. Above this were two small knots that did nicely for eyes. The Sawhorse was the favorite steed of Ozma and to prevent its wooden legs from wearing out she had them shod with plates of gold.

Jack said "Good morning" to the Sawhorse and placed upon the creature's back a saddle of purple leather, studded with jewels.

"Where now?" asked the horse, blinking its knot eyes at Jack.

"We're going to rescue two babes in the wood," was the reply. Then he climbed into the saddle and the wooden animal pranced out of the stable, through the streets of the

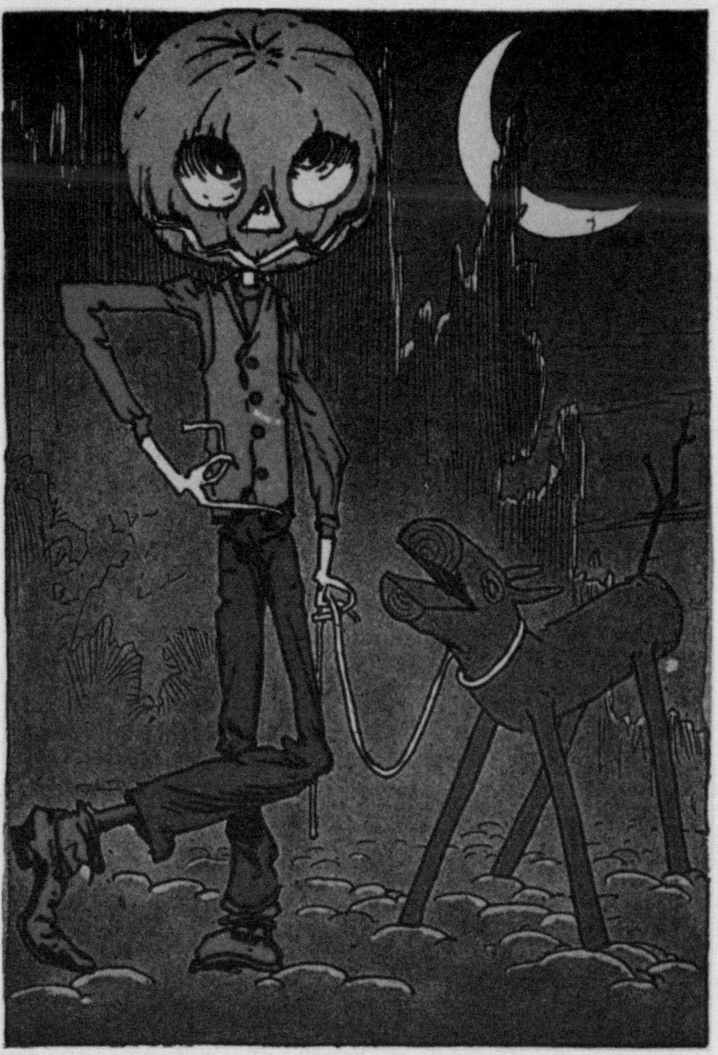

Emerald City and out upon the highway leading to the western forest where the children were lost.

Small though he was, the Sawhorse was swift and untiring. By nightfall they were in the far west and quite close to the forest they sought. They passed the night standing quietly by the roadside. They needed no food, for their wooden bodies never became hungry; nor did they sleep, because they never tired. At daybreak they continued their journey and soon reached the forest.

Jack now examined the map Ozma had given him and found the right path to take, which the Sawhorse obediently followed. Underneath the trees all was silent and gloomy and Jack beguiled the way by whistling gayly as the Sawhorse trotted along.

The paths branched so many times and in so many different ways that the Pumpkinhead was often obliged to consult Ozma's map, and finally the Sawhorse became suspicious.

"Are you sure you are right?" it asked.

"Of course," answered Jack. "Even a Pumpkinhead whose brains are seeds can follow so clear a map as this. Every path is plainly marked, and here is a cross where the children are."

Finally they reached a place, in the very heart of the forest, where they came upon the lost boy and girl. But they found the two children bound fast to the trunk of a big tree, at the foot of which they were sitting.

When the rescuers arrived, the little girl was sobbing bitterly and the boy was trying to comfort her, though he was probably frightened as much as she.

"Cheer up, my dears," said Jack, getting out of the saddle. "I have come to take you back to your parents. But why are you bound to that tree?"

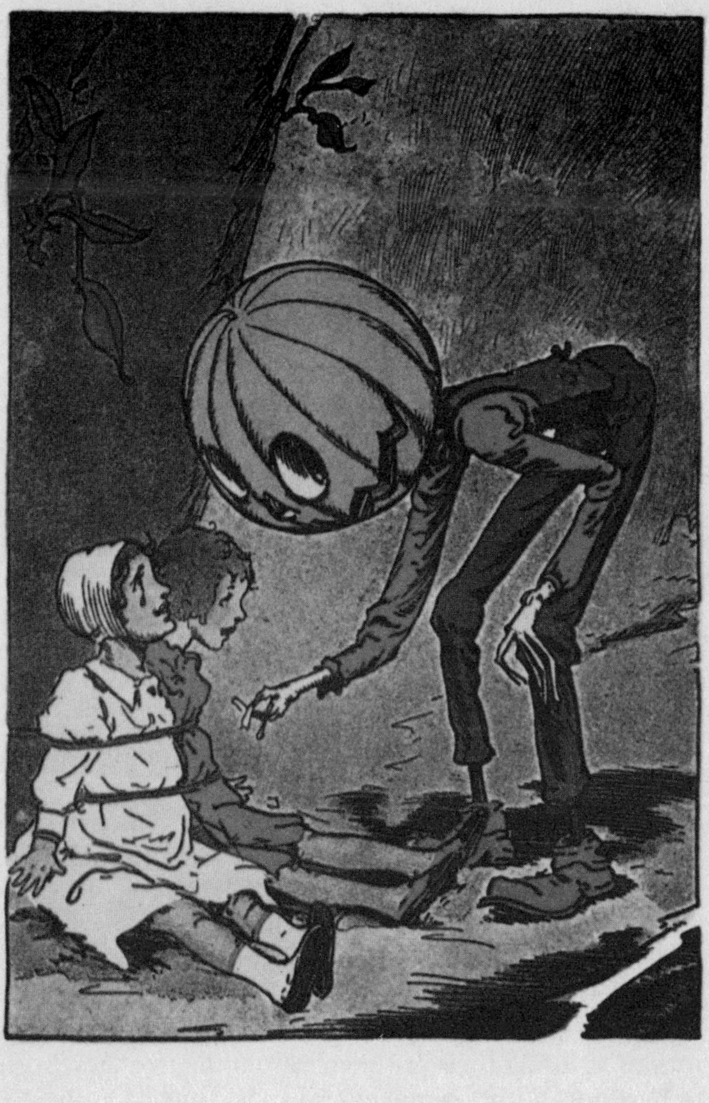

"Because," cried a small, sharp voice, "they are thieves and robbers. That's why!"

"Dear me!" said Jack, looking around to see who had spoken. The voice seemed to come from above.

A big gray squirrel was sitting upon a low branch of the tree. Upon the squirrel's head was a circle of gold, with a diamond set in the center of it. He was running up and down the limbs and chattering excitedly.

"These children," continued the squirrel, angrily, "robbed our storehouse of all the nuts we had saved up for winter. Therefore, being the King of all the Squirrels in this forest, I ordered them arrested and put in prison, as you now see them. They had no right to steal our provisions and we are going to punish them."

"We were hungry," said the boy, pleadingly, "and we found a hollow tree full of nuts, and ate them to keep alive. We didn't want to starve when there was food right in front of us."

"Quite right," remarked Jack, nodding his pumpkin head. "I don't blame you one bit, under the circumstances. Not a bit."

Then he began to untie the ropes that bound the children to the tree.

"Stop that!" cried the King Squirrel, chattering and whisking about. "You mustn't release our prisoners. You have no right to."

But Jack paid no attention to the protest. His wooden fingers were awkward and it took him some time to untie the ropes. When at last he succeeded, the tree was full of squirrels, called together by their King, and they were furious at losing their prisoners. From the tree they began to hurl nuts at the Pumpkinhead, who laughed at them as he helped the two children to their feet.

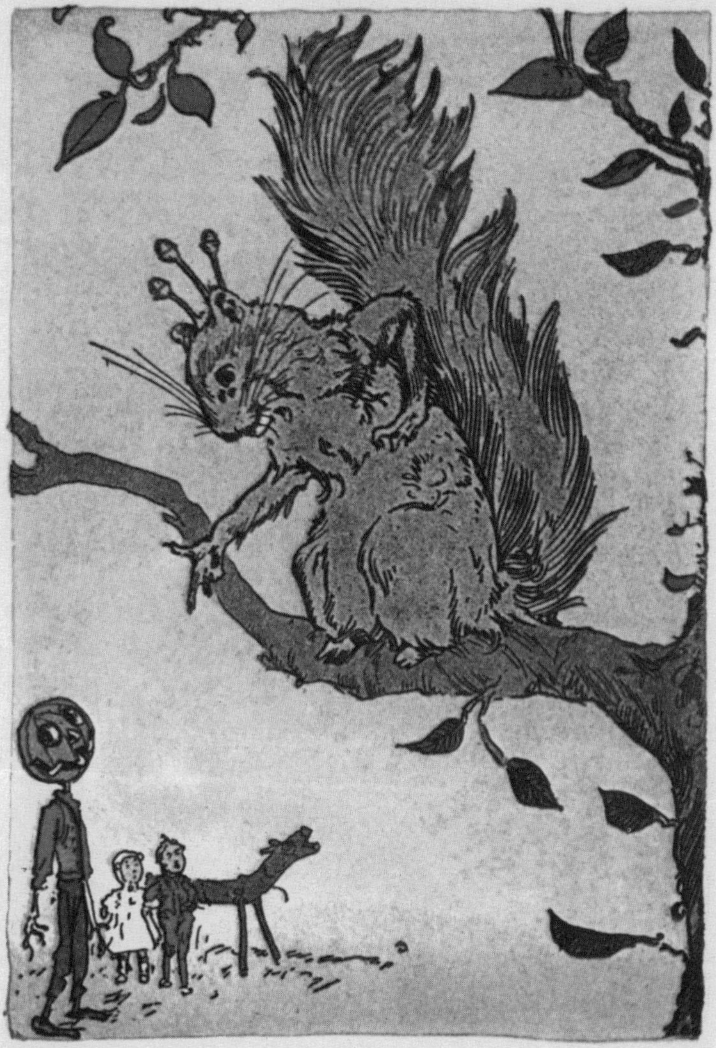

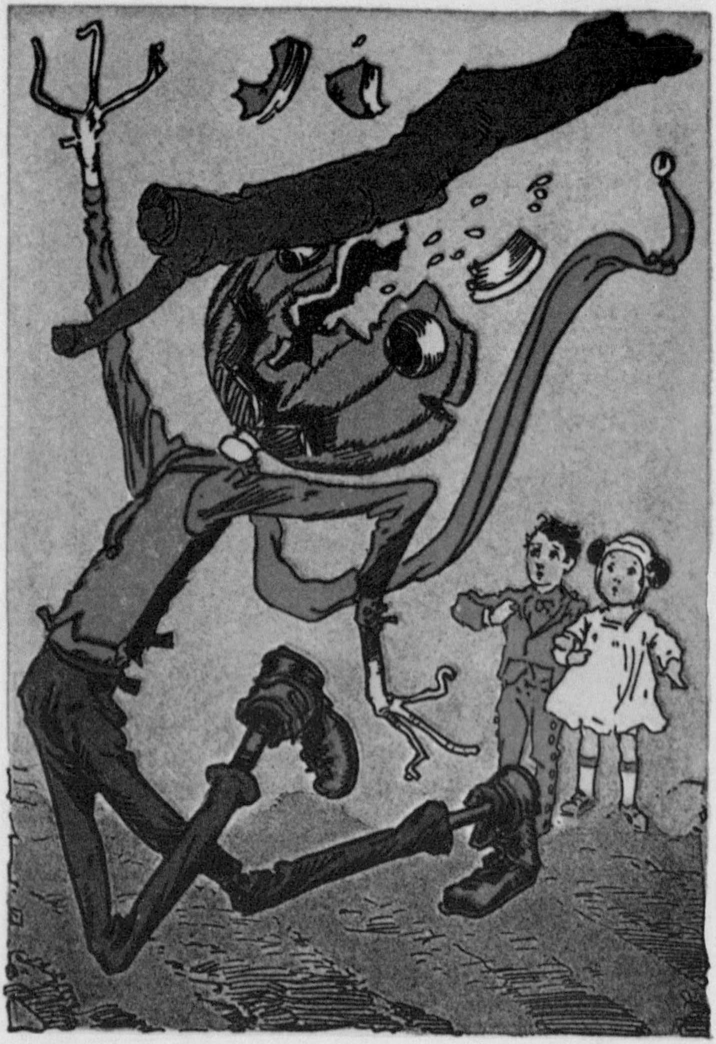

Now, at the top of this tree was a big dead limb, and so many squirrels gathered upon it that suddenly it broke away and fell to the ground. Poor Jack was standing directly under it and when the limb struck him it smashed his pumpkin head into a pulpy mass and sent Jack's wooden form tumbling, to stop with a bump against a tree a dozen feet away.

He sat up a moment afterward, but when he felt for his head it was gone. He could not see; neither could he speak. It was perhaps the greatest misfortune that could have happened to Jack Pumpkinhead, and the squirrels were delighted. They danced around in the tree in great glee as they saw Jack's plight.

The boy and girl were indeed free, but their protector was ruined. The Sawhorse was there, however, and in his way he was wise. He had seen the accident and knew that the smashed pumpkin would never again serve Jack as a head. So he said to the children, who were frightened at this accident to their newfound friend:

"Pick up the Pumpkinhead's body and set it on my saddle. Then mount behind it and hold it on. We must get out of this forest as soon as we can, or the squirrels may capture you again. I must guess at the right path, for Jack's map is no longer of any use to him since that limb destroyed his head."

The two children lifted Jack's body, which was not at all heavy, and placed it upon the saddle. Then they climbed up behind it and the Sawhorse immediately turned and trotted back along the path he had come, bearing all three with ease. However, when the path began to branch into many paths, all following different directions, the wooden animal became puzzled and soon was wandering aimlessly about, without any hope of finding the right way. Toward evening

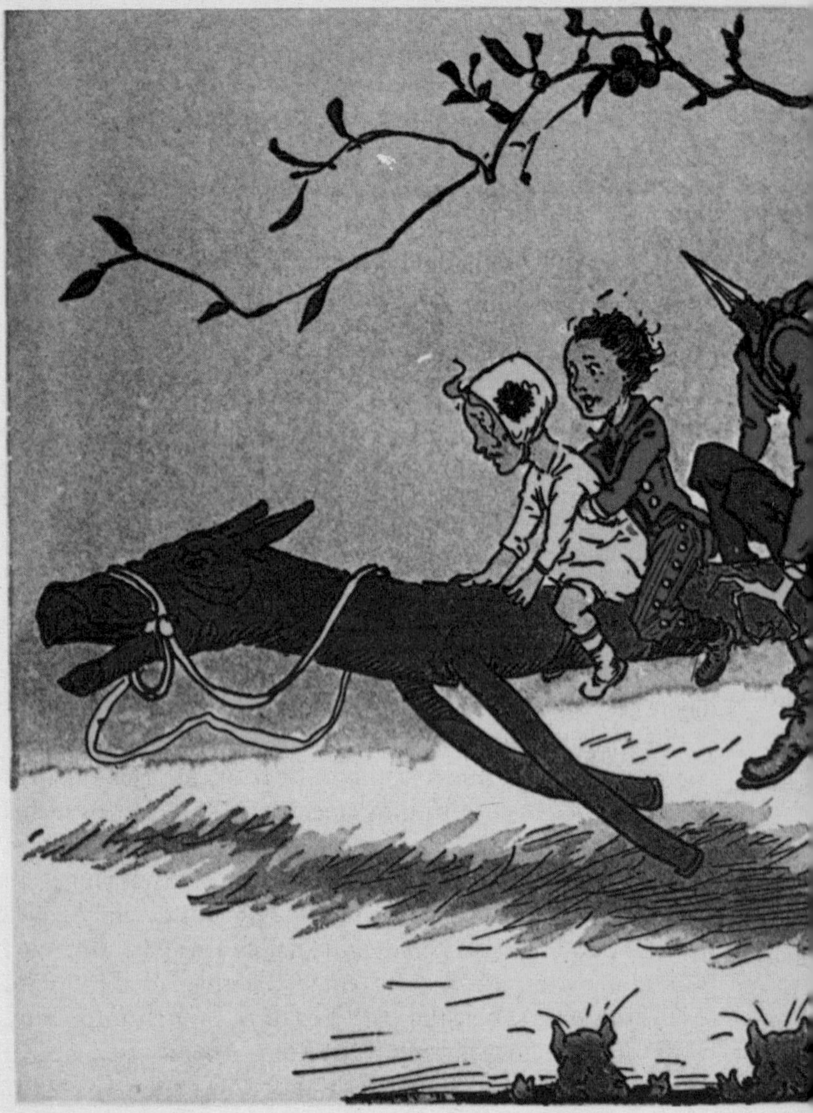

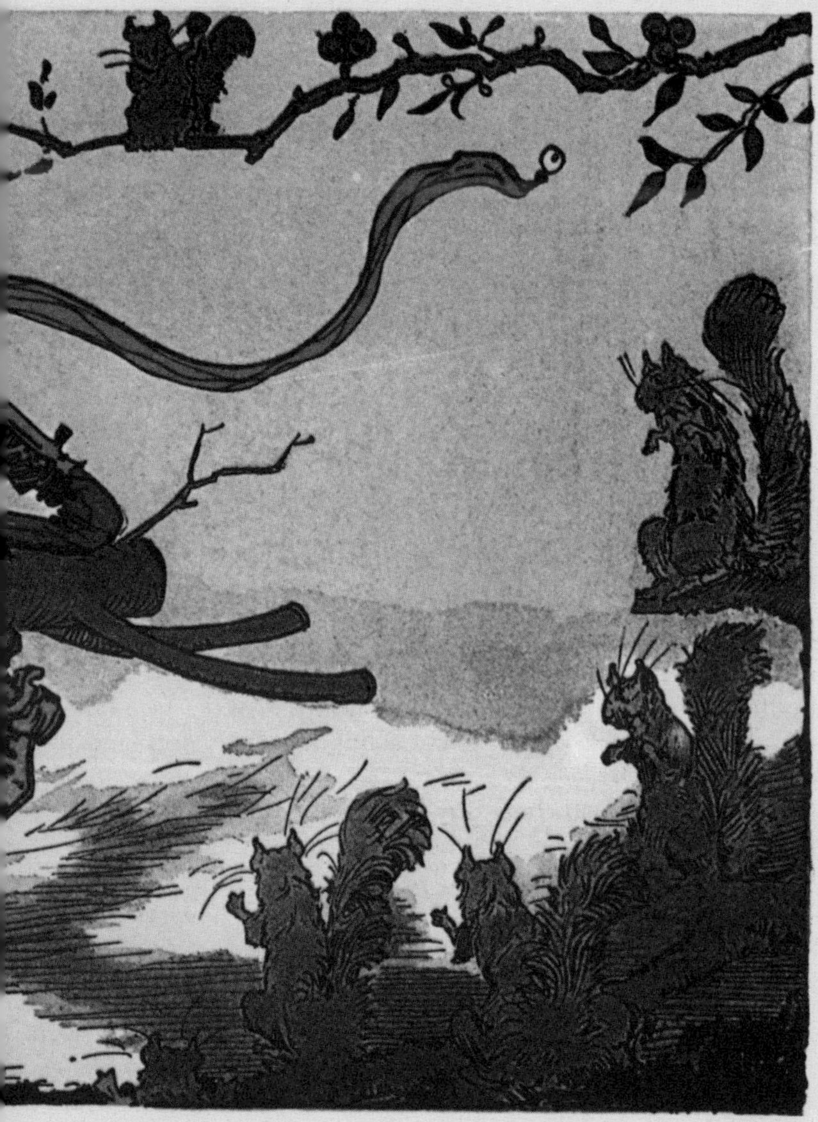

they came upon a fine fruit tree, which furnished the children a supper, and at night the little ones lay upon a bed of leaves while the Sawhorse stood watch, with the limp, headless form of poor Jack Pumpkinhead lying helpless across the saddle.

Now, Ozma had seen in her Magic Picture all that happened in the forest, so she sent the little Wizard, mounted upon the Cowardly Lion, to save the unfortunates. The Lion knew the forest well and when he reached it he bounded straight through the tangled paths to where the Sawhorse was wandering, with Jack and the two children on his back.

The Wizard was grieved at the sight of the headless Jack, but believed he could save him. He first led the Sawhorse out of the forest and restored the boy and girl to the arms of their anxious friends, and then he sent the Lion back to Ozma to tell her what had happened.

The Wizard now mounted the Sawhorse and supported Jack's form on the long ride to the pumpkin field. When they arrived at Jack's house the Wizard selected a fine pumpkin—not too ripe—and very neatly carved a face on it. Then he stuck the pumpkin solidly on Jack's neck and asked him:

"Well, old friend, how do you feel?"

"Fine!" replied Jack, and shook the hand of the little Wizard gratefully. "You have really saved my life, for without your assistance I could not have found my way home to get a new head. But I'm all right, now, and I shall be very careful not to get this beautiful head smashed." And he shook the Wizard's hand again.

"Are the brains in the new head any better than the old ones?" inquired the Sawhorse, who had watched Jack's restoration.

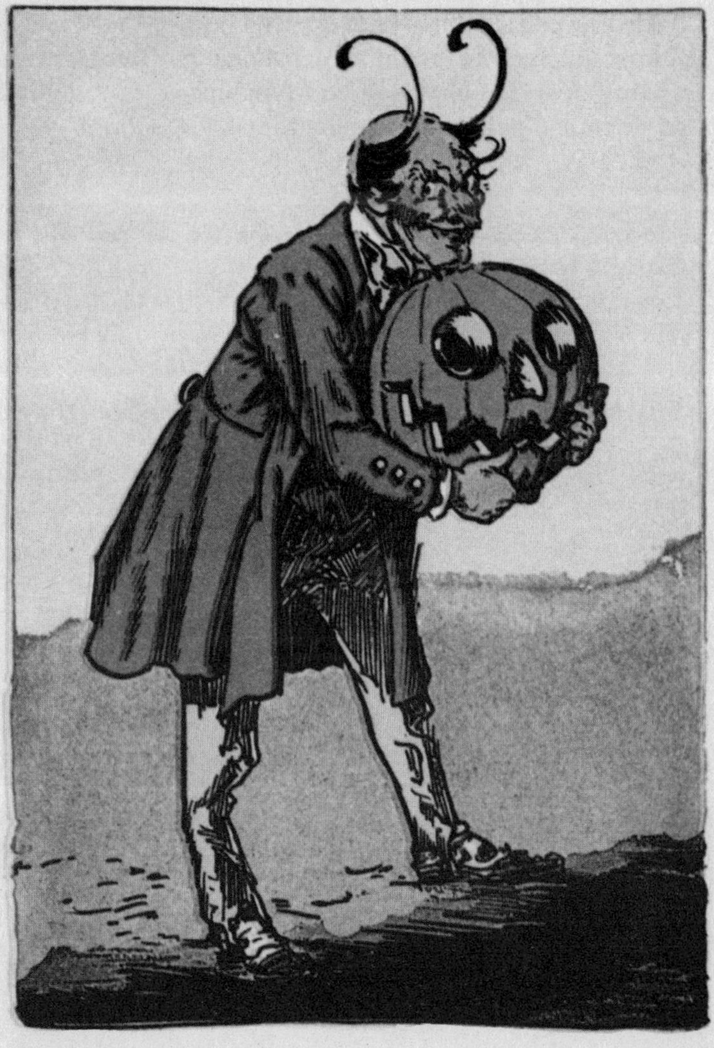

"Why, these seeds are quite tender," replied the Wizard, "so they will give our friend tender thoughts. But, to speak truly, my dear Sawhorse, Jack Pumpkinhead, with all his good qualities, will never be noted for his wisdom."

THE SCARECROW
and
THE TIN WOODMAN

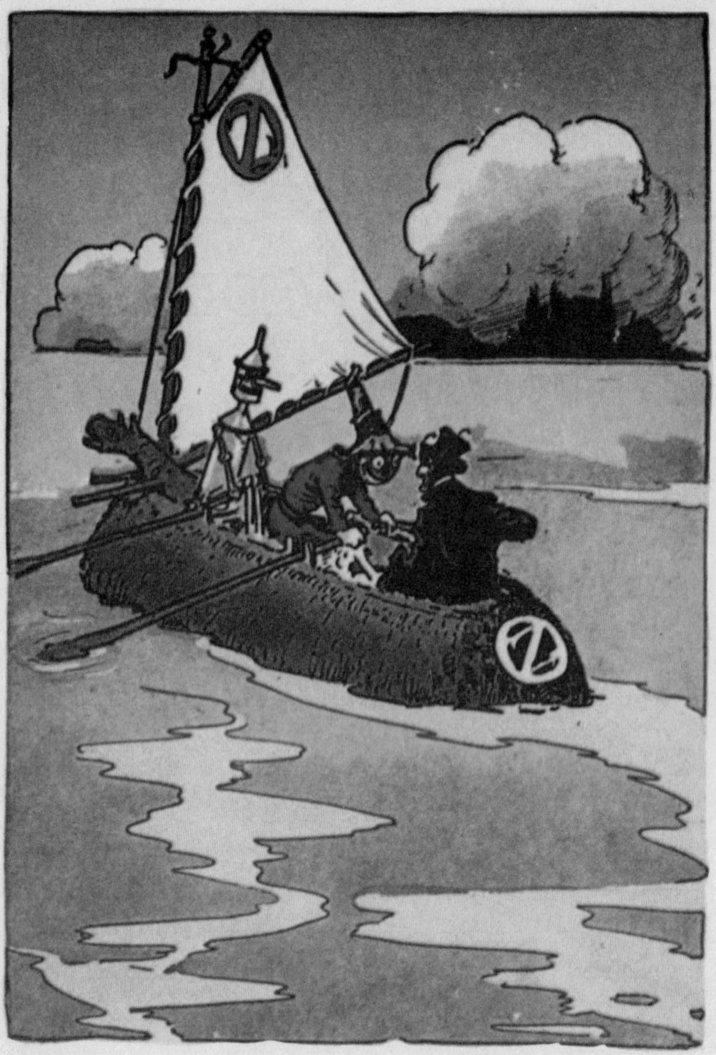

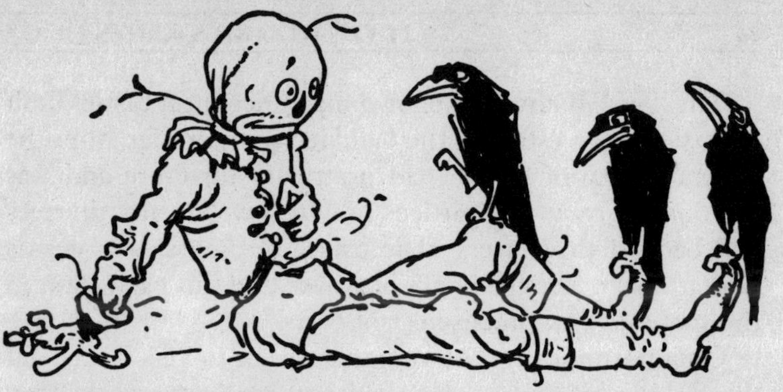

THE SCARECROW AND THE TIN WOODMAN

THERE lived in the Land of Oz two queerly made men who were the best of friends. They were so much happier when together that they were seldom apart; yet they liked to separate, once in a while, that they might enjoy the pleasure of meeting again.

One was a Scarecrow. That means he was a suit of blue Munchkin clothes, stuffed with straw, on top of which was fastened a round cloth head, filled with bran to hold it in shape. On the head were painted two eyes, two ears, a nose and a mouth. The Scarecrow had never been much of a success in scaring crows, but he prided himself on being a superior man, because he could feel no pain, was never tired, and did not have to eat or drink. His brains were sharp, for the Wizard of Oz had put pins and needles in the Scarecrow's brains.

The other man was made all of tin, his arms and legs and head being cleverly jointed so that he could move them freely. He was known as the Tin Woodman, having at one time been a woodchopper, and everyone loved him because the Wizard had given him an excellent heart of red plush.

The Tin Woodman lived in a magnificent tin castle, built on his country estate in the Winkie Land, not far from the Emerald City of Oz. It had pretty tin furniture and was surrounded by lovely gardens in which were many tin trees and beds of tin flowers. The palace of the Scarecrow was not far distant, on the banks of a river, and this palace was in the shape of an immense ear of corn.

One morning the Tin Woodman went to visit his friend the Scarecrow, and as they had nothing better to do they decided to take a boat ride on the river. So they got into the Scarecrow's boat, which was formed from a big corncob, hollowed out and pointed at both ends and decorated around the edges with brilliant jewels. The sail was of purple silk and glittered gayly in the sunshine.

There was a good breeze that day, so the boat glided swiftly over the water. By and by they came to a smaller river that flowed out from a deep forest, and the Tin Woodman proposed they sail up this stream, as it would be cool and shady beneath the trees of the forest. So the Scarecrow, who was steering, turned the boat up the stream and the friends continued talking together of old times and the wonderful adventures they had met with while traveling with Dorothy, the little Kansas girl. They became so much interested in this talk that they forgot to notice that the boat was now sailing through the forest, or that the stream was growing more narrow and crooked.

Suddenly the Scarecrow glanced up and saw a big rock just ahead of them.

"Look out!" he cried; but the warning came too late.

The Tin Woodman sprang to his feet just as the boat bumped into the rock, and the jar made him lose his balance. He toppled and fell overboard and being made of tin

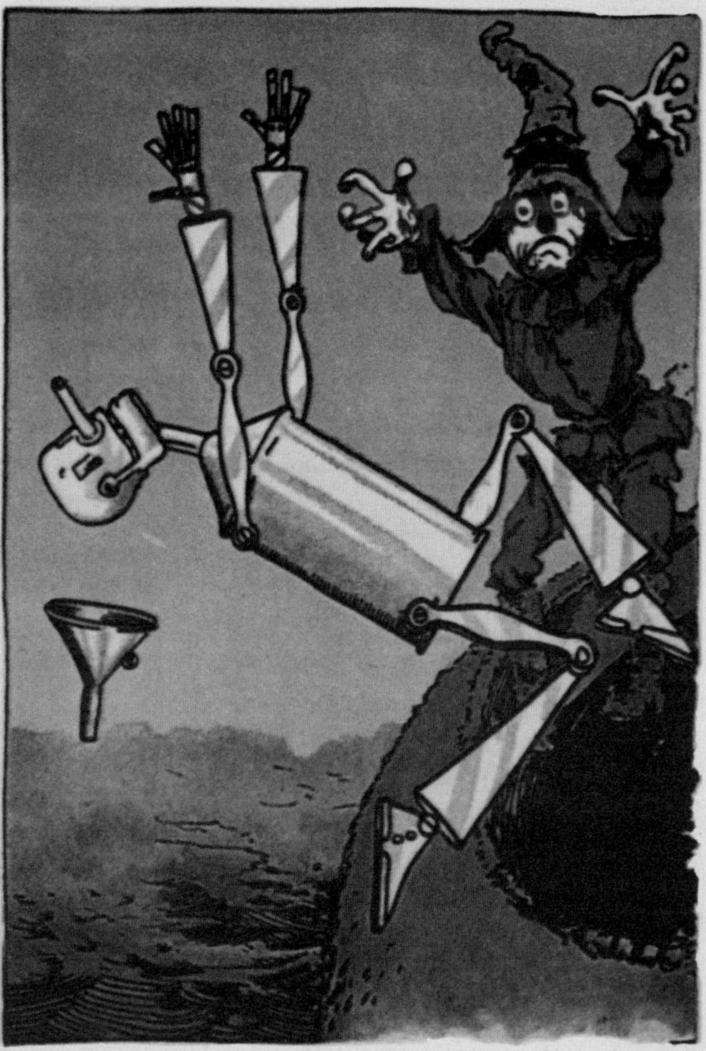

he sank to the bottom of the water in an instant and lay there at full length, face up.

Immediately the Scarecrow threw out the anchor, so as to hold the boat in that place, and then he leaned over the side and through the clear water looked at his friend sorrowfully.

"Dear me!" he exclaimed; "what a misfortune."

"It is, indeed," replied the Tin Woodman, speaking in muffled tones because so much water covered him. "I cannot drown, of course, but I must lie here until you find a way to get me out. Meantime, the water is soaking into all my joints and I shall become badly rusted before I am rescued."

"Very true," agreed the Scarecrow; "but be patient, my friend, and I'll dive down and get you. My straw will not rust, and is easily replaced, if damaged, so I'm not afraid of the water."

The Scarecrow now took off his hat and made a dive from the boat into the water; but he was so light in weight that he barely dented the surface of the stream, nor could he reach the Tin Woodman with his outstretched straw arms. So he floated to the boat and climbed into it, saying the while:

"Do not despair, my friend. We have an extra anchor aboard, and I will tie it around my waist, to make me sink, and dive again."

"Don't do that!" called the tin man. "That would anchor you also to the bottom, where I am, and we'd both be helpless."

"True enough," sighed the Scarecrow, wiping his wet face with a handkerchief; and then he gave a cry of astonishment, for he found he had wiped off one painted eye and now had but one eye to see with.

"How dreadful!" said the poor Scarecrow. "That eye must have been painted in watercolor, instead of oil. I must

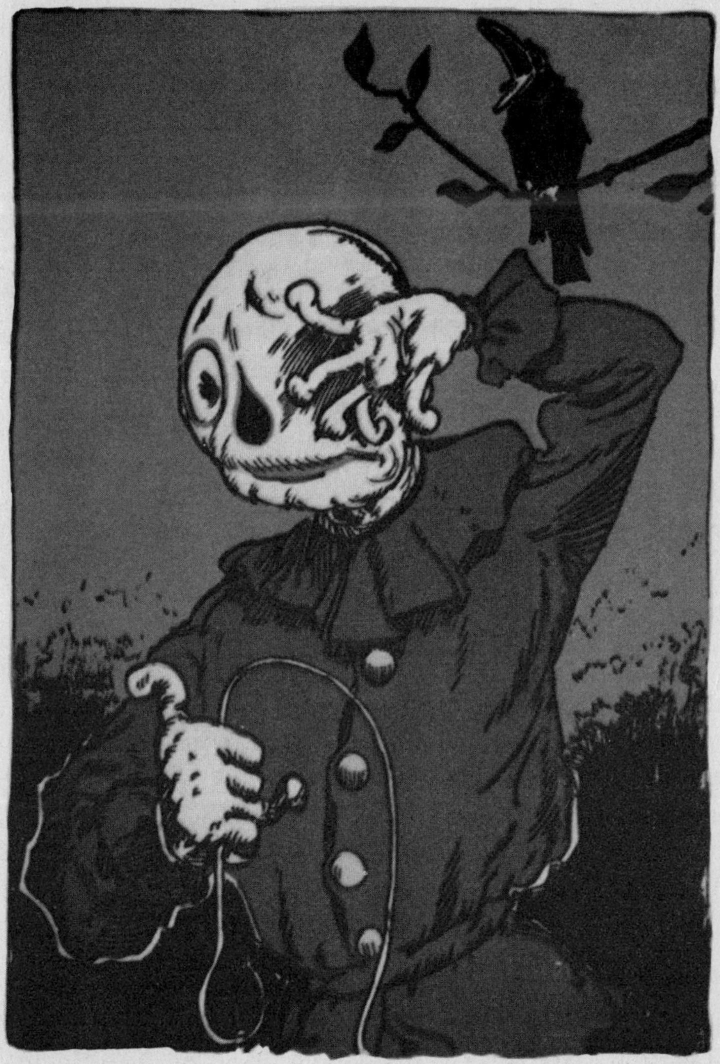

be careful not to wipe off the other eye, for then I could not see to help you at all."

A shriek of elfish laughter greeted this speech and looking up the Scarecrow found the trees full of black crows, who seemed much amused by the straw man's one-eyed countenance. He knew the crows well, however, and they had usually been friendly to him because he had never deceived them into thinking he was a meat man—the sort of man they really feared.

"Don't laugh," said he; "you may lose an eye yourselves, some day."

"We couldn't look as funny as you, if we did," replied one old crow, the king of them. "But what has gone wrong with you?"

"The Tin Woodman, my dear friend and companion, has fallen overboard and is now on the bottom of the river," said the Scarecrow. "I'm trying to get him out again, but I fear I shall not succeed."

"Why, it's easy enough," declared the old crow. "Tie a string to him and all of my crows will fly down, take hold of the string, and pull him up out of the water. There are hundreds of us here, so our united strength could lift much more than that."

"But I can't tie a string to him," replied the Scarecrow. "My straw is so light that I am unable to dive through the water. I've tried it, and knocked one eye out."

"Can't you fish for him?"

"Ah, that is a good idea," said the Scarecrow. "I'll make the attempt."

He found a fishline in the boat, with a stout hook at the end of it. No bait was needed, so the Scarecrow dropped the hook into the water till it touched the Woodman.

"Hook it into a joint," advised the crow, who was now

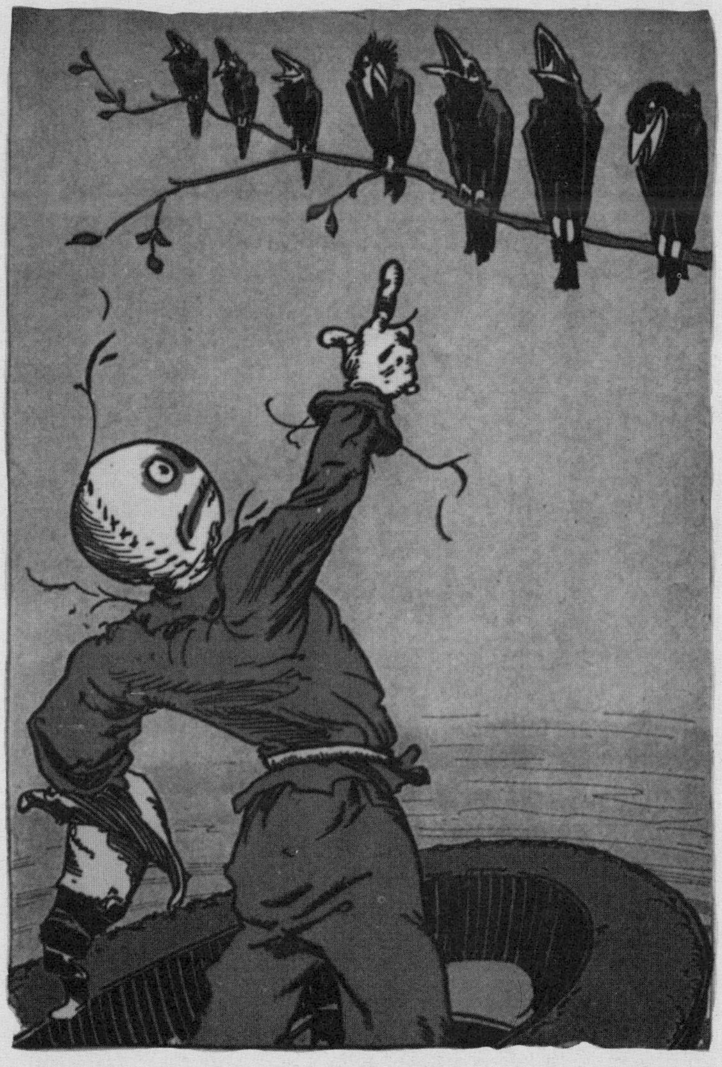

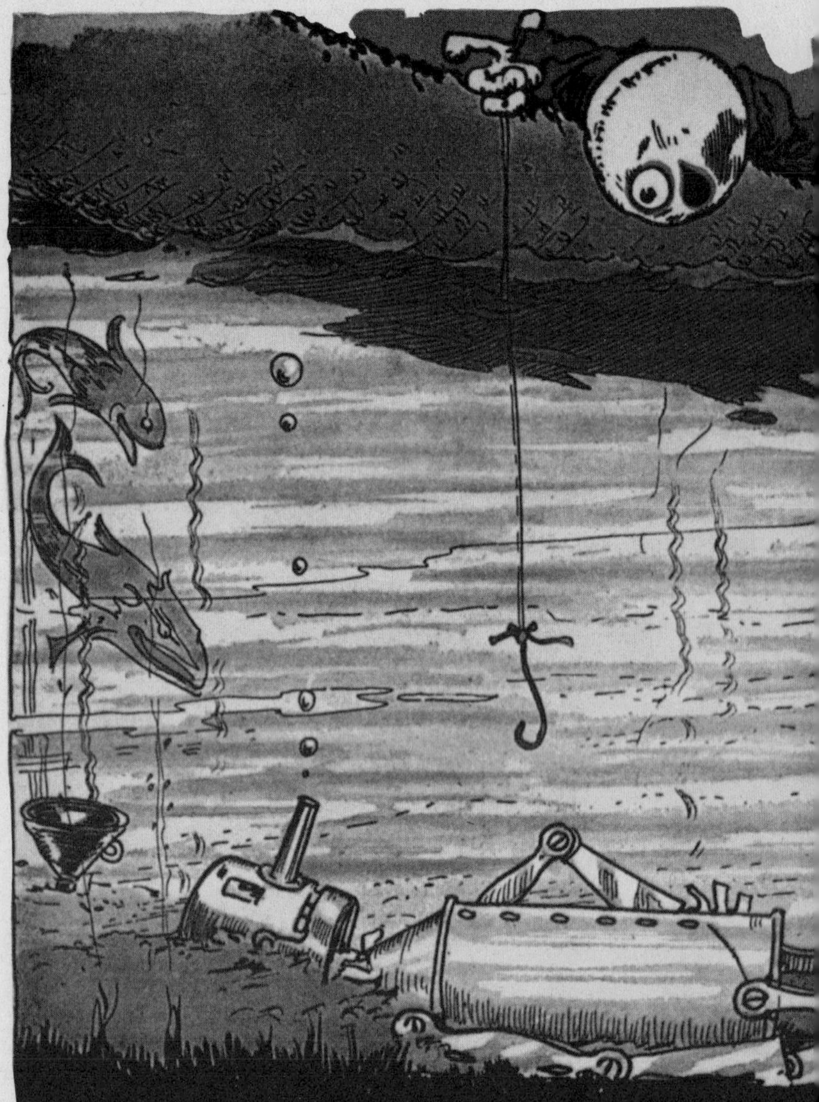

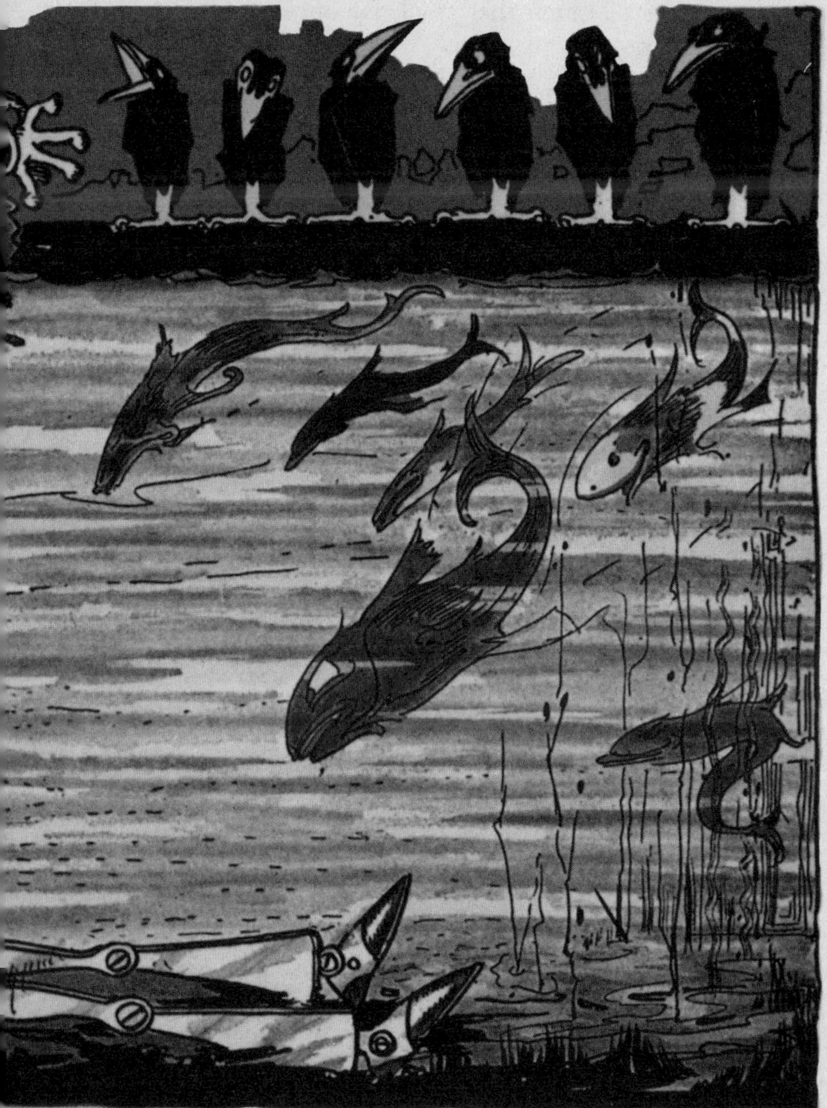

perched upon a branch that stuck far out and bent down over the water.

The Scarecrow tried to do this, but having only one eye he could not see the joints very clearly.

"Hurry up, please," begged the Tin Woodman; "you've no idea how damp it is down here."

"Can't you help?" asked the crow.

"How?" inquired the tin man.

"Catch the line and hook it around your neck."

The Tin Woodman made the attempt and after several trials wound the line around his neck and hooked it securely.

"Good!" cried the King Crow, a mischievous old fellow. "Now, then, we'll all grab the line and pull you out."

At once the air was filled with black crows, each of whom seized the cord with beak or talons. The Scarecrow watched them with much interest and forgot that he had tied the other end of the line around his own waist, so he would not lose it while fishing for his friend.

"All together for the good caws!" shrieked the King Crow, and with a great flapping of wings the birds rose into the air.

The Scarecrow clapped his stuffed hands in glee as he saw his friend drawn from the water into the air; but next moment the straw man was himself in the air, his stuffed legs kicking wildly; for the crows had flown straight up through the trees. On one end of the line dangled the Tin Woodman, hung by the neck, and on the other dangled the Scarecrow, hung by the waist and clinging fast to the spare anchor of the boat, which he had seized hoping to save himself.

"Hi, there—be careful!" shouted the Scarecrow to the

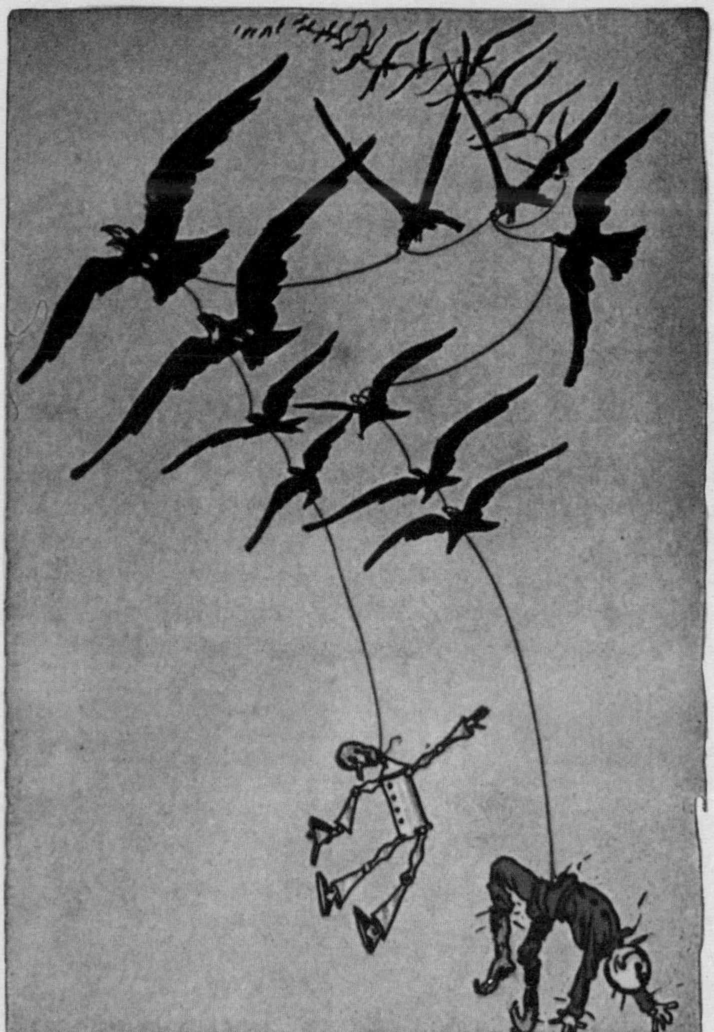

crows. "Don't take us so high. Land us on the river bank."

But the crows were bent on mischief. They thought it a good joke to bother the two, now that they held them captive.

"Here's where the crows scare the Scarecrow!" chuckled the naughty King Crow, and at his command the birds flew over the forest to where a tall dead tree stood higher than all the other trees. At the very top was a crotch, formed by two dead limbs, and into the crotch the crows dropped the center of the line. Then, letting go their hold, they flew away, chattering with laughter, and left the two friends suspended high in the air—one on each side of the tree.

Now the Tin Woodman was much heavier than the Scarecrow, but the reason they balanced so nicely was because the straw man still clung fast to the iron anchor. There they hung, not ten feet apart, yet unable to reach the bare tree-trunk.

"For goodness' sake don't drop that anchor," said the Tin Woodman anxiously.

"Why not?" inquired the Scarecrow.

"If you did I'd tumble to the ground, where my tin would be badly dented by the fall. Also you would shoot into the air and alight somewhere among the tree-tops."

"Then," said the Scarecrow, earnestly, "I shall hold fast to the anchor."

For a time they both dangled in silence, the breeze swaying them gently to and fro. Finally the tin man said: "Here is an emergency, friend, where only brains can help us. We must think of some way to escape."

"I'll do the thinking," replied the Scarecrow. "My brains are the sharpest."

He thought so long that the tin man grew tired and tried

to change his position, but found his joints had already rusted so badly that he could not move them. And his oil-can was back in the boat.

"Do you suppose your brains are rusted, friend Scarecrow?" he asked in a weak voice, for his jaws would scarcely move.

"No, indeed. Ah, here's an idea at last!"

With this the Scarecrow clapped his hands to his head, forgetting the anchor, which tumbled to the ground. The result was astonishing; for, just as the tin man had said, the light Scarecrow flew into the air, sailed over the top of the tree and landed in a bramble-bush, while the tin man fell plump to the ground, and landing on a bed of dry leaves was not dented at all. The Tin Woodman's joints were so rusted, however, that he was unable to move, while the thorns held the Scarecrow a fast prisoner.

While they were in this sad plight the sound of hoofs was heard and along the forest path rode the little Wizard of Oz, seated on a wooden Sawhorse. He smiled when he saw the one-eyed head of the Scarecrow sticking out of the bramble-bush, but he helped the poor straw man out of his prison.

"Thank you, dear Wiz," said the grateful Scarecrow. "Now we must get the oil-can and rescue the Tin Woodman."

Together they ran to the river bank, but the boat was floating in midstream and the Wizard was obliged to mumble some magic words to draw it to the bank, so the Scarecrow could get the oil-can. Then back they flew to the tin man, and while the Scarecrow carefully oiled each joint the little Wizard moved the joints gently back and forth until they worked freely. After an hour of this labor the Tin Woodman was again on his feet, and although still a little stiff he managed to walk to the boat.

The Wizard and the Sawhorse also got aboard the corn-cob craft and together they returned to the Scarecrow's palace. But the Tin Woodman was very careful not to stand up in the boat again.

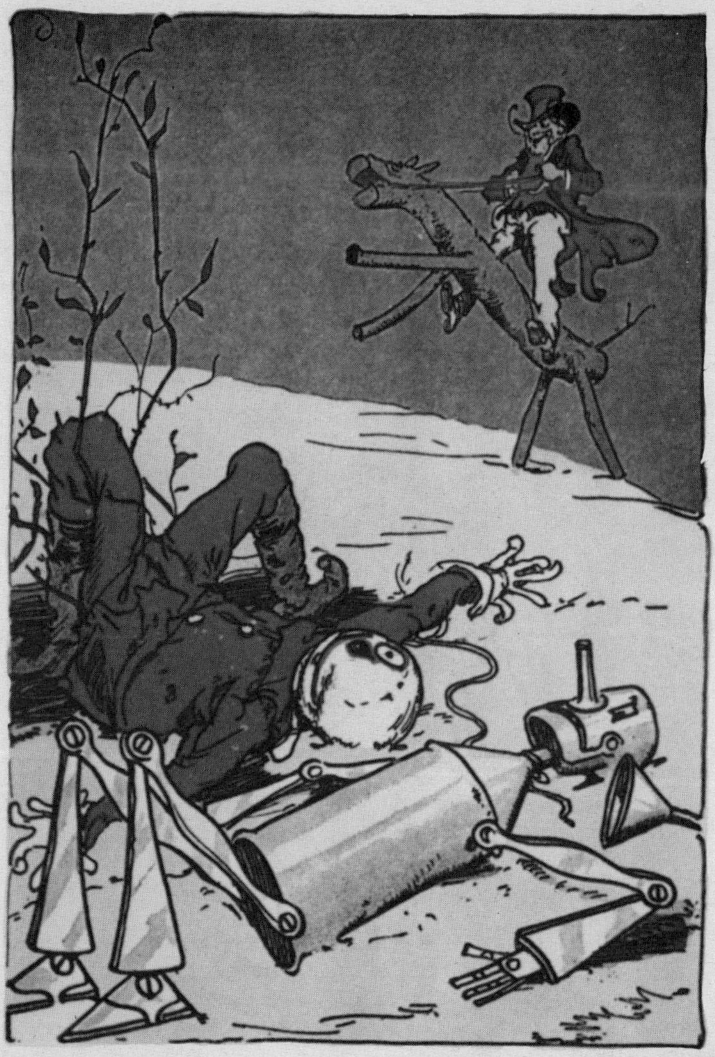

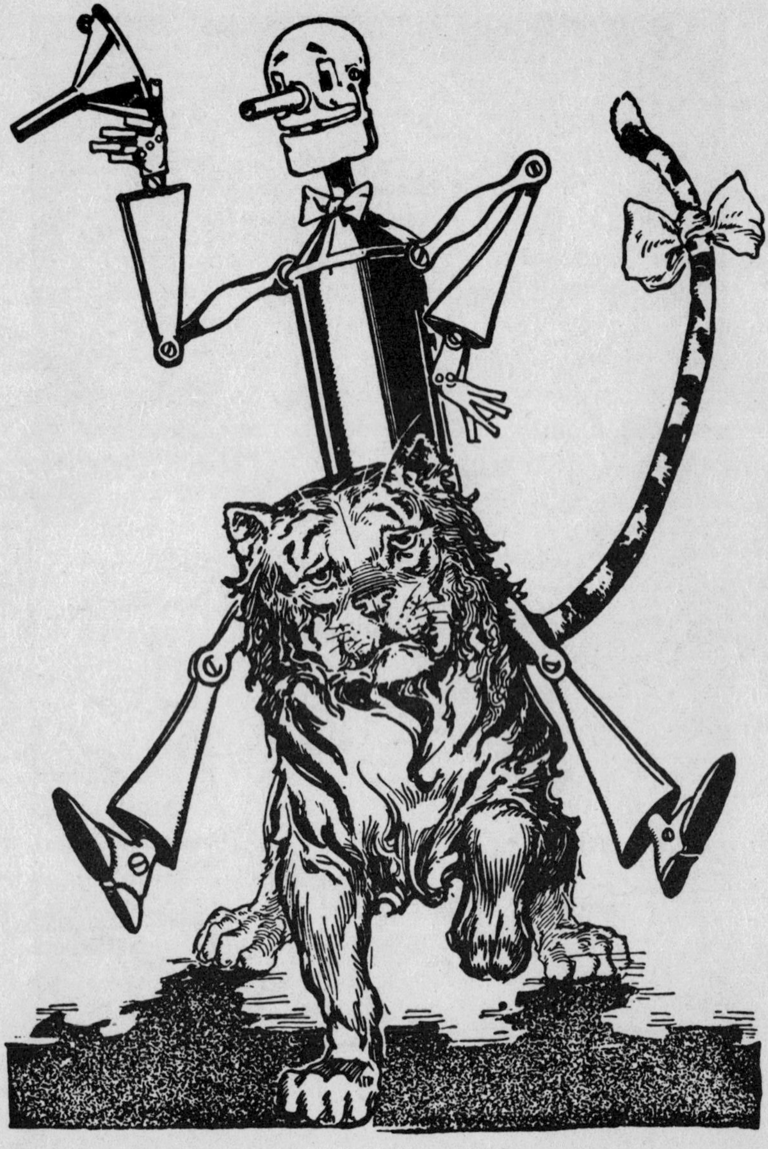

ABOUT THE CONTRIBUTORS

L. FRANK BAUM first published *The Wonderful Wizard of Oz* in 1900, and it quickly became the best-selling children's book of the year. Baum went on to write more popular Oz titles like *The Marvelous Land of Oz*, *The Emerald City of Oz*, and *The Patchwork Girl of Oz*.

A highly prolific author, Baum wrote many other fairy tales, including *The Sea Fairies* and *Sky Island*. His book with W.W. Denslow, *Father Goose, His Book* (1899), is considered the first distinctively American children's picture book. In 1914, in response to countless letters from children, Baum wrote this collection of tales for younger children featuring the best-loved characters from Oz.

JOHN R. NEILL was a young Philadelphia newspaper cartoonist at the time this collection was first published. He illustrated all of the Oz books but the original one.

MICHAEL PATRICK HEARN is an avid Oz collector, and owns such memorabilia as his prized first edition of *The Wonderful Wizard of Oz*, as well as letters, posters, photographs, and other items connected with Baum, his illustrators, and other collaborators. Hearn's *The Annotated Wizard of Oz* is considered the first thorough critical consideration of Baum and his work. His most recent book is *The Porcelain Cat* (Little, Brown), and he's currently hard at work on a full-length biography of "the Royal Historian of Oz," L. Frank Baum.

Can Science Be Fun?
You Bet, With Mr. Rose!

Meet Sally, Matt, Jennifer, and the rest of the fun-loving members of Mr. Rose's science class. Mr. Rose sure knows how to make learning fun and exciting for his class—and for *you*, too! Each book has loads of drawings, plus terrific activities you can do at home.

☐ TRIP DAY
On a visit to a pond, the class collects mud, water, and rocks to bring back to the classroom. You can follow along with the class as they learn how to use a microscope and magnifying glass. There are hundreds of different creatures living in just a drop of water!   15618-7 $2.50/$2.95 in Canada

☐ PET DAY
The class helps Mr. Rose build a home for their desert pets. Learn about the habits of lizards, gerbils—even a kangaroo rat! See how much fun it can be to hold a tiny mouse! 15620-9 $2.50/$2.95 in Canada

☐ WORM DAY
Are worms yucky? Find out how they move and if they like water. When the class asks questions about where worms live, Mr. Rose takes them all outside on a worm-hunting expedition!   15619-5 $2.50/$2.95 in Canada

On Sale: August 1988